A COLLEGE GUY?

This could be interesting, thought Danielle. But before she could say anything, the doorbell rang.

"That's probably Jack." Christine got up and hurried into the front hall to answer the door.

This is it, Danielle thought. Her chance to show up Teresa and Heather by actually snagging a college guy. If Christine's friend was even half as cute as the Yale boys they'd seen this afternoon, Teresa and Heather would be drooling with envy. *Please don't be a nerd*, Danielle prayed.

"Oh, hi, Jack! Come on in," said Christine.

Danielle kept her gaze riveted to the entryway, her heart beating triple time in anticipation. Christine appeared in the doorway first. But behind her was a guy who could only be described as . . . completely and utterly divine!

Merivale Mall

JUNIOR WEEKEND

by Jana Ellis

Troll Associates

Library of Congress Cataloging in Publication Data

Ellis, Jana.
    Junior weekend.

    (Merivale mall; #6)
    Summary: Lori and Danielle's weekend on a college
campus and bittersweet experiences with college men
indicate that youth is a time to get to know many
different people.
    [1. Cousins—Fiction.   2. Dating (Social customs)
—Fiction]   I. Title.   II. Series: Ellis, Jana.
Merivale mall; #6.
PZ7.E472Ju   1989   [Fic]   88-19988
ISBN 0-8167-1364-2 (pbk.)

A TROLL BOOK, published by Troll Associates,
Mahwah, NJ 07430

JUNIOR WEEKEND

CHAPTER ONE

"I am *not* in love with Don James!"

Sixteen-year-old Danielle Sharp tossed her long auburn hair over her shoulder and frowned at her two best friends. "I just happened to run into him a couple of times and it was entirely by *accident!*"

Heather Barron and Teresa Woods giggled even harder. "Oh, come *on*, Danielle," Heather murmured, examining her perfectly manicured fingernails. "You don't have to pretend with us."

"Yeah," Teresa agreed. "We *did* see those pictures of you two together. You know—the ones where you and Don just happen to be staring dreamily into each other's eyes?" She batted her long eyelashes for dramatic effect.

"Come on, face it, Danielle. You and Don have it *bad* for each other!" Heather's voice rang embarrassingly loudly across the mall's open first-floor plaza.

Teresa's mouth turned up in a catlike grin. In another instant she and Heather burst into hysterical laughter again, practically falling off the mall's polished wood bench.

Danielle could feel herself blushing. Ever since Teresa and Heather had found the snapshots of her with Don, they had teased her mercilessly. Whenever she saw them in the Atwood Academy cafeteria, one of them would call out, "How's *Don*, Danielle?" making sure the next table over could hear perfectly. Now the whole school was gossiping about Danielle and her new "grease-monkey" boyfriend!

It was all positively ridiculous! Danielle had been out with Don just that one time. But Teresa and Heather wouldn't let her live it down!

Seething inside, Danielle licked her frozen yogurt cone in silence and ignored her friends. But that was pretty difficult when they simply wouldn't stop laughing. "Oh, please," she finally said. "Don't you have anything better to talk about?" She lowered her eyelids and gave her friends a sly glance with her devastating green eyes. "For instance, *your* love lives?"

Heather's laughter evaporated into silence, and suddenly they seemed very, *very* interested in their own yogurt cones. *Score one for me*, Danielle thought triumphantly. Right now neither Heather nor Teresa had a whole lot happening in the love department, and it was kind of a sore spot with them.

Actually, Danielle had to admit that Don

was an interesting topic of conversation—he certainly had a lot more going for him than most of the guys at Atwood. Don was sort of rough around the edges—the strong, silent type—and never afraid to take a dare. But he had a hidden side, too, a thoughtfulness and a gentleness that always surprised Danielle. And because he lived on his own, he seemed a lot older than other guys, even though he was only seventeen. Not to mention that he was totally gorgeous, in a tough, dark way.

As Don's handsome face filled Danielle's thoughts, she had to feel a little sorry that a real relationship between the two of them was, in fact, utterly impossible. After all, she was Danielle Sharp of Wood Hollow Hills, the wealthiest neighborhood in Merivale, and one of exclusive Atwood Academy's most popular juniors. She had to live up to the super-high status her family had achieved ever since her father had made a fortune designing and developing Merivale Mall. She had to wear the best clothes, go to the best schools . . . and date the best boys.

And Don James? He lived on a run-down farm with a bunch of guys who wore grungy black leather jackets and drove around like maniacs on motorcycles. Don went to public school—Merivale High School—and studied auto mechanics, of all things. In other words, Don was the very definition of low status! So even though he was gorgeous, smart, and crazy about Danielle, he had too many strikes against him for her even to consider dating him. Sure, she *liked* him. But she couldn't afford to let on to Teresa and Heather about that. Not in a million years. Because if she did, she could kiss her whole classy, refined reputation good-by—forever!

But Danielle's friends just wouldn't let up. "It's okay, Danielle." Heather shrugged. "We understand. You just can't resist a guy with grease under his fingernails."

Danielle bit her tongue to keep herself from saying something equally mean to Heather. She couldn't risk making either of her friends *too* mad. The fact was, when she'd transferred from Merivale High to Atwood, they had been the only popular girls who even talked to her. And thanks to them, Danielle had been able to work her way into the popular crowd too. She was afraid that if she ever did anything to make them mad, it would be all over.

Danielle racked her brain for a way to change the subject without being too obvious, but she couldn't come up with anything.

"Hey!" Heather suddenly exclaimed. She sat up straight, looking at something on the other side of the mall. "Check out these guys," she said, gesturing discreetly in their direction with her head.

Danielle and Teresa instantly swiveled to gaze across the airy plaza. They weren't disappointed. There, walking out of Aunti Pasta's, were three of the best-looking guys Danielle had ever seen. A bulldog's mug was emblazoned across each of their blue and white jackets, and the single word *Yale* was written in large letters on the back.

"College guys," said Teresa breathlessly.

"I've got the one on the right," added Heather. "He's gorgeous."

"Fan-tastic," echoed Danielle. Finally she and her friends had something they could agree on. "The other two aren't bad either. Three of us, three of them."

"They must be visiting," said Teresa. "I know they don't live here—we'd have noticed them before. I wonder who they're staying with—"

"It's a shame it isn't me." Heather sighed.

"Well, I'm getting a visitor from college this weekend," Danielle teased, delicately tossing the rest of her cone into the trash can next to her. "A sophomore."

Teresa raised an eyebrow and looked at her friend. "Oh?"

"Unfortunately, it's only my sister, Christine," Danielle said, suppressing a giggle. "She's coming home for the weekend."

"Funny, I always forget you *have* a sister," Heather said.

Heather and Teresa had never met Christine because she had graduated from Merivale High. She could have transferred to Atwood when their father had gotten rich, but she'd wanted to finish school with her classmates. Danielle didn't really understand, and it was too complicated to explain to her Atwood friends why her sister had gone to public school. So as a result she simply didn't mention Christine too much.

"Does your sister have a boyfriend, Danielle?" Teresa wanted to know. She crunched into the last of her yogurt cone, following the Yale guys with her gaze.

Danielle rolled her eyes. "She says she's too busy studying to get involved with anyone. Can you believe it?"

As Heather and Teresa let out a nasty giggle, Danielle felt a flash of annoyance shoot through her. Even though she couldn't always understand her sister, she did admire her, and she hated listening to her friends laugh at Christine. Her sister was hard-working, smart, and very loving. On top of that, she had always been totally gorgeous—she'd inherited their mother's high cheekbones and devastatingly long eyelashes.

As a kid, Danielle had spent more than one sleepless night wondering if she would ever be as beautiful as Christine. Well, she was now— thank goodness—and she'd never have to wonder again.

"I wish *I* had an older sister so I could meet some college guys," Teresa said as the Yale boys ambled across the plaza, then stopped to look at something in Hobart Electronics' window.

"Me too," said Heather. "They *are* fabulous, aren't they?" She stared at the handsome threesome.

"They're so sophisticated," Teresa agreed with a nod.

"And mature—" added Heather.

"And, let's face it—unavailable," said Danielle. "We're stuck with Atwood boys until we go away to school. But I know something that will make us all feel better. Facades awaits!"

A little shopping at Merivale Mall's most expensive boutique was always good for the soul. Besides, Danielle was due for some new, elegant, totally ravishing outfit—especially since Christine would undoubtedly look terrific, and Danielle didn't want to listen to her mother making comparisons between her daughters.

With one last glance at the Yale boys, she and her friends headed toward Facades.

Lori Randall instantly spotted Patsy Donovan moving toward her through the crowd of people in front of the SixPlex movie theater. The giant chocolate-chip-cookie-shaped hat on Patsy's head would have stood out anywhere.

Poor Patsy! thought Lori, trying not to laugh. Why did the Cookie Connection make their employees wear such ridiculous outfits?

But glancing at her own orange nylon outfit with the fluorescent yellow bib apron, Lori had to admit that the Tio's Tacos uniforms weren't much better. And she had to wear a black hair net over her long blond hair while she was at work too. Oh, well, it was all part of having a job.

"Hi, Lori. What's going on?" Patsy's face lit up as she hurried over to her friend. "Ann couldn't make it—she's still doing sit ups." Their other friend, Ann Larson, worked as an aerobics instructor at the Body Shoppe. The three girls had a standing agreement to meet up in the main plaza during their breaks from work. Ten minutes didn't give them much time to talk, but Lori guessed it was better than nothing.

"Not much is happening, really," Lori said. "I've been working a whole lot this week. That's about it."

"You know, I was just thinking that you never told me what Professor Mortenson said about your designs the other day." The well-known teacher from the Fashion Institute had been in Merivale judging the Miss Merivale Mall beauty pageant—a pageant Patsy herself had won!—and Lori had taken the opportunity to get his opinion on her own clothing designs. Designing had always been Lori's passion. But just recently she'd begun to realize that it could be her career too.

Lori and Patsy started to walk down the center promenade of the mall, edging their way through the crowds of shoppers. "For starters, he said a lot of the work I had in my portfolio was really original. And he said the Fashion Institute would be a good school for me—"

"That's great!" Patsy exclaimed, her hazel eyes shining.

"I *was* pretty thrilled," Lori admitted. "He

talked to me for almost an hour—told me all about the school, and the different kinds of degrees I could go for."

"So did you already get into the Fashion Institute, or what?"

Lori shrugged. "Well, he didn't exactly say that, but I think I have a good chance. He also told me to look at some other colleges and universities, too, because design is such a big field. There's a lot more to it than fashion."

"Like what?" Patsy asked.

"Well, I could be a stylist for commercials, or a lighting designer in the theater, or even a furniture designer. It's all so exciting, Patsy. I just can't wait to go to college!"

Patsy laid a meaningful hand on Lori's wrist. "Did he say anything about a scholarship?" she asked. "I mean, not that you aren't making a fortune selling tacos," she joked.

Lori laughed. "He said I had a good chance with that, too, if I went after the right scholarships —he even gave me a list of them!" Lori pulled a piece of folded paper from the pocket of her apron. *"Voilà!"*

"Lori, I'm so happy for you!" Patsy said with a grin.

"The only bad part is going to be leaving Nick," Lori mused, almost to herself. "I mean, I finally have a boyfriend who I really love, and than *wham!*—I'm off to college."

"Oh, don't worry about that *now*. You won't

be leaving Nick for another year and a half."
Patsy waved her hand dismissively.

"I know I'm being silly. But when it does happen, I know I'll miss him terribly."

Lori shivered slightly at the thought. Just imagining it made her want to go right over to Nick's family's store, Hobart Electronics, and give him a huge kiss. Whenever he put his strong, muscular arms around her, Lori had to pinch herself to make sure she wasn't dreaming. Nick Hobart—the sweetest, most handsome, most sensitive guy in the entire world—had picked *her* out of all the other girls in Merivale. The past couple of months with him had been sheer bliss. Lori just couldn't imagine saying good-by. She sighed.

Patsy gave her friend a sympathetic look. The two girls came to a stop in front of Tio's neon storefront. "Hey, want to come over to my house later, or are you going out with Nick?"

"No, I'm not," Lori answered, brushing off her uniform and preparing to get back to work. "Actually, you won't believe this, but I'm going over to Danielle's house."

Patsy arched one eyebrow and looked at Lori as if she had lost her mind. "Your snobby cousin's?" she asked. "What's the occasion? Why did Princess Dani invite you to Windsor Castle? I thought only royalty were allowed."

Lori smiled. Deep down, Danielle wasn't the complete prig Patsy made her out to be, but Lori couldn't blame her for thinking it. Danielle

and her friends had never been too nice to
Patsy, especially before she'd lost all that weight
and won the Miss Merivale Mall Contest.

"Oh, no, it's not Danielle who invited
me—of course," Lori answered. "Actually, her
mother asked the whole family over. My cousin,
Christine, is coming home from Kensington College, so Aunt Serena decided to have a little
friendly get-together."

"Really? I don't know Christine, but I've
seen her—she's even prettier than Danielle. But
if they're anything alike, I feel sorry for you."

Lori laughed. "Actually, pretty much the
only thing they *do* have in common is their
looks. As far as her personality goes, Christine's really down-to-earth. I think you'd like
her a lot."

"Maybe," Patsy agreed. "Well, if I don't
get going, I'll be late to work. Have fun tonight
—if you can. Be sure to tell Danielle I *didn't* say
hello." Patsy waved good-by and hurried off
down the promenade.

As Lori stepped into Tio's, she decided she'd
better keep Patsy's comment to herself. Lori
did love her cousin, but she had to admit,
Danielle was pretty difficult to get along with—
even when she *wasn't* mad. The last thing Lori
wanted to do was add fuel to the fire.

CHAPTER TWO

Turning her white BMW onto the circular drive, Danielle hoped Christine had made it ahead of her. That way, she wouldn't have to face her mother on her own. But the only car in the drive was the Premier Caterer's van. Danielle's mother hated to cook but she loved to throw dinner parties—and Premier always made her look like the perfect chef. And if a guest happened to ask for a recipe, Mrs. Sharp would look at her, smile sweetly, and say she couldn't give away *all* her little secrets.

Danielle parked the car and stepped out. Maybe Christine took the train home, she thought.

Danielle hated to admit it, but ever since her sister had gone away to Kensington she had been terribly lonely at home. Her mother never really talked to her. All she did was harp about moving to New York or Philadelphia so she could mingle with "the right sort of people." And her father was determined to stay in Merivale, working a hundred hours a week so he wouldn't have to listen to his wife's complaints.

And when he *was* at home, it was always the same old shouting and arguing between her parents. For years Danielle and Christine had listened to it together, but now, without her sister around, Danielle had to face it all alone.

So when Danielle walked through their family's elegant foyer and into the living room, she was thrilled to see Christine and her mother chatting cozily together. Or, at least as cozily as Serena Sharp ever got. Even now, alone at home, her mother was impeccably dressed in a beige silk pants suit. She was pouring tea for the two of them from an antique silver tea service.

Christine, on the other hand, looked fantastic, even in her slightly faded blue jeans and an ancient T-shirt. "Hey, Christine!" Danielle cried.

"Dani!" Christine called out. She jumped up from the couch and gave her sister a warm hug. "How are you? You look great!"

"Why she insists on wearing that jump suit I have absolutely no idea," Mrs. Sharp commented acidly. "It's just not right for a high school girl."

Who asked you? Danielle wrinkled her nose imperceptibly as she and her sister settled back into the couch.

Mrs. Sharp handed Christine a cup of tea. "The sugar's right here, dear. Doesn't your sister look wonderful, Danielle?" she asked, turning toward her with a smile.

"Yes, she does," Danielle admitted. With her coppery hair and azure eyes, Christine could have made cover girl on any one of a dozen fashion magazines.

"Just lovely," Mrs. Sharp gushed. "College has done wonders for you, Christine. Maybe you'll even find yourself a nice young man."

"Mom," Christine sighed. She threw Danielle a glance that said, *Here we go again.*

"Well," said Mrs. Sharp, "you can't let your youth and beauty slip away, you know."

"I'm only nineteen!" Christine protested. "I have lots of time to find a boyfriend."

Danielle loved Christine, but she couldn't help feeling a twinge of pleasure when her mother gave her sister a hard time. It helped to make up for all the millions of times she'd heard, "Christine is *such* a good student. She's *so* responsible. Christine doesn't let *her* car get run down. Christine keeps *her* things tidy."

Danielle knew her sister was smarter and more together than she was. But did her mother have to rub it in all the time?

"So, dear. Have you arranged it so you can stay for a couple of days?" asked Mrs. Sharp.

"Just until tomorrow, Mom. I came with a friend who was going home for the weekend, too, and since Merivale was on his way, he offered to drop me off."

"He? Anyone interesting?" Mrs. Sharp pasted an innocent smile on her face.

"He's a *friend*, Mom. That's all. I met him in my psychology class when we teamed up for a research project. As a matter of fact, I asked him to stop in and meet you—he's just out getting gas right now. I'd like to have him over for dinner before he drives the rest of the way home, if that's okay with you."

A college guy for dinner? This could be interesting, thought Danielle. *Come on, Mom. Say yes,* she begged silently.

But instead, Serena Sharp bit her lip and frowned. "I don't know, darling. I ordered only for seven. And—if he's just a friend—"

"Fine. Whatever you say." Christine turned to Danielle, rolling her eyes. Their mother was being difficult, as usual. Danielle smiled at her sister's exasperated expression. It was great having Christine back to share the little annoyances.

"So how's life at Atwood?" Christine asked, moving closer to Danielle on the couch.

"Pretty good. Except for the boy situation. There just isn't anyone interesting left who I haven't already dated—" answered Danielle. Before she could say anything more, the doorbell rang.

"That's probably the guy I was talking about," said Christine. She got up and hurried into the front hall to answer the door.

This is it, Danielle thought. Her chance to show up Teresa and Heather by actually snagging a college guy. If Christine's friend was even half as cute as the Yale boys they'd seen this afternoon,

Teresa and Heather would be drooling with envy. *Please don't be a nerd*, Danielle prayed.

"Oh, hi, Jack! Come on in." Danielle heard her sister say.

Danielle kept her gaze riveted to the entryway, her heart beating triple time in anticipation. Christine appeared through the doorway first. But behind her was a guy who could be described only as—completely and utterly gorgeous!

"Mom, this is Jack Aldrich. Jack, my mother—" Christine introduced. Danielle blinked and tried to regain her composure.

Jack was about six feet tall, with wavy dark hair, and he had the most amazing face Danielle had ever seen. Stunning hazel eyes stood out above handsomely high cheekbones. His nose looked as though it had been chiseled by a sculptor. And that body! Muscular, but not *too* much. Toned yet lean. A gray tweed jacket—an *expensive* one, Danielle noted—was slung jauntily over one of Jack's strong, broad shoulders.

"How do you do, Mrs. Sharp?"

Jack extended his hand politely to Danielle's mother. His hazel eyes radiated confidence.

Mrs. Sharp stood up and shook hands eagerly. "It's nice to meet you, Jack," she said warmly, taking in his winning appearance and obviously approving of what she saw.

"And this is my little sister, Danielle," Christine said. "She's a junior in high school."

Why, oh, why, did Christine have to put it

that way? Now Jack would think Danielle was a kid!

But when he said hello there wasn't a trace of condescension in his voice. "Hi. I've heard a lot about you."

"Nothing bad, I hope," Danielle responded in her lowest and most sophisticated voice. She threw a warning glace at Christine.

"Oh, you can be sure it wasn't!" Jack answered quickly. Danielle couldn't help but notice the charmed gleam in his eyes. His gaze seemed to say, *How come I haven't met you before?*

Well, why not? Danielle decided. She was as pretty as any college girl—except possibly Christine.

"Jack, have a seat," Christine offered, gesturing toward the antique love seat.

"Oh, please do! So, where are you from, Jack?" Mrs. Sharp asked curiously as Jack made himself comfortable.

"Philadelphia. Main Line," he replied casually, tossing off the name of Philadelphia's most elite community as if it were just another neighborhood.

Jack Aldrich . . . Main Line—slowly, a connection was forming in Danielle's mind. Jack Aldrich . . . the Aldrich Corporation . . . if she was right, Jack's wealth went as far back in time as the Florida land boom and as far into the future as Aldrich Space Technologies could take it!

And from the look on Serena Sharp's face, it was clear that the same thought had crossed *her* mind. "Uh, what do your parents do?" It wasn't often that Danielle had seen her mother use such tact, but she was certainly doing a good job of it now.

"They run a company," Jack explained. "The Aldrich Corporation, actually," he confessed modestly.

A look of greedy delight passed over Serena Sharp's face for just an instant. "Well, you must be *famished* after such a long trip!" she said, suddenly the one-hundred-percent-perfect hostess. "I'll have Grace bring out some hors d'oeuvres."

"Thank you, Mrs. Sharp, but that's not necessary. I'll get dinner at a coffee shop before I drive home."

"A coffee shop?" Serena looked from Jack to Christine with a look of puzzled innocence. "But you must dine with us!"

"Well, I wouldn't want to impose. I know Christine doesn't get home that often—"

"Don't be silly," Mrs. Sharp scolded gently. "We can visit with both of you during dinner. Besides, how can you pass up Brie and pâté for a cheeseburger and onion rings?"

Christine smiled at Jack. "We'd love you to stay."

Boy, would we! Danielle said to herself.

"Absolutely!" her mother agreed. "I insist!"

"Well, since you put it that way," Jack replied, "I'd love to stay for dinner. It'll be a pleasure."

Fantastic, Danielle thought. For once in her life, her mother had saved the day.

"I wish I didn't have to go out now," said Christine wistfully. "But I promised my friend Kate I'd stop by and see her."

"It's good to keep up with old friends," Jack commented. He smiled politely. Then he turned to Danielle. "Just like it's important to make new ones."

Danielle felt as if she were going to explode. He meant *her*. This handsome, charming, *rich* college guy was actually interested in her! It was a good thing she'd cut her afternoon shopping short after all.

"Let me tell Grace to put out an extra place setting right now," said Mrs. Sharp, standing. "By the way, Jack, I hope you won't mind, but some of our relatives will be coming to dinner. Christine, I knew Aunt Cynthia and Uncle George would want to see you."

"Of course I don't mind. More people just means more fun, right?" Jack said.

Not when it's the Randalls, Danielle thought. Her cousin Lori's family was nice enough—that wasn't the point. Lori herself had certainly helped Danielle out of some pretty sticky situations. Like the time Danielle had gone over on her credit card allowance and Lori had lent her the money she'd saved to buy that old jalopy of a car. But face it, Lori and her whole family were just plain boring. And that was *not* the type of company Danielle wanted around for her one big chance to be with Jack Aldrich.

"Great! I'd love to see the Randalls," exclaimed Christine. "Are Lori and the boys coming too?"

"Lori is, but the boys have a scout meeting," Mrs. Sharp replied. "Well, see you kids later. I have some preparing to do in the kitchen," she announced, smiling at Jack as she left the room.

Preparing! The only thing Danielle's mother needed to do for dinner was tell Premier Caterers to make it eight for dinner instead of seven.

"I've got to go too." Christine stood up and threw her Fair Isle sweater over her shoulder. "If I don't meet Kate soon, I won't be back in time for dinner." She sighed. "Sorry to leave you like this, Jack. Could you show him around a little, Danielle?"

"Sure, Christine," Danielle purred as her sister made her way to the front hall. *I'll be happy to take him off your hands!* she added silently.

"See you later, Christine," Jack called. Then he turned to Danielle. "Ready to give me the grand tour?"

Am I ever! she thought. What incredible luck that her older sister had discovered such a major hunk. More than that, how great that Jack and Christine were just friends! That left him free, completely free, for Danielle herself.

"Come on, Jack." She beamed, laying her hand familiarly on his own. "Let me show you around."

CHAPTER THREE

Jack stepped back into the skylit living room and Danielle guided him to the couch. "Well, that's it—the whole house," she said with a shrug. She inched just a fraction closer to him. "My dad's going to put in a billiard room downstairs one of these days."

"This is a great house," Jack said, looking out through the huge picture window and across the luscious green of the front lawn.

"It's okay. There are nicer estates down the road." *Our place probably looks like a guest house compared to the Aldrich estate*, Danielle thought, suddenly embarrassed.

"Oh, I don't think they *could* be any nicer." Jack smiled enchantingly. "Besides, you have a real home here, you know? Huge places can get very lonely. I think this house is just right."

Jack was so tactful. Danielle decided it was his charm that she liked best about him—besides his eyes, his face, his body, his sophistication, his money. . . .

"I'm so glad your mother asked me to dinner." Jack put down his empty ginger ale glass on the end table and looked directly at Danielle.

A little shiver wormed its way down Danielle's spine. What chemistry! She could tell by the way Jack was watching her that he felt it too.

"Would you like some more ginger ale, Jack?" she purred. "I can get it for you—"

"No, don't go to any trouble," he remarked. "Thanks, though."

"It's no trouble at all. Besides," she hinted, "any friend of Christine's is a . . . friend of mine." She flashed Jack another one of her devastating smiles.

Danielle was soaring. Handsome, older Jack Aldrich had walked into her life—and practically into her arms! He liked her! She was sure of it!

"I'm really glad I met your sister," he said, moving closer on the couch and looking straight into her eyes. "You look a lot alike, you know that?"

He paused, suddenly looking almost shy. Danielle didn't move. She barely breathed. Something was about to happen—she could feel it! He was either going to say how much he liked her, or he was going to kiss her. . . .

"I wanted to ask you—" he began.

Crunch, crunch, crunch. The loud, harsh sound of a car pulling into the Sharps' graveled driveway ripped the perfect moment to bits. Unconsciously, Jack moved away from Danielle just a hair. Danielle suppressed an irritated frown. "That's probably my aunt and uncle," she said with fake brightness. "They're always early."

How annoying, when she'd just been getting cozy with Jack. On top of it all, they were probably showing up in their old Dodge Dart. When were they going to get a new car, Danielle wondered—this century, or the next? It was going to be so embarrassing when Jack noticed.

Danielle leaned back in the couch and looked out the window as the car stopped at the front steps. Her aunt stepped out of the car just as Lori did, and then her uncle came around the front of the car to join them. Danielle had to admit that Lori looked pretty in her straight, long black skirt and waist-length red cardigan sweater.

Pretty but—sort of boring. Danielle herself intended to wow Jack with an enticing miniskirt and top ensemble she'd just picked up at Facades. Still, it was too bad they'd have to get stuck making polite chitchat with the Randalls. It would have been *so* much nicer to spend the evening alone.

"Is your cousin in college too?" Jack asked, staring out the window.

Danielle bristled. "No, she's my age. We hardly ever see each other, though. She doesn't go to Atwood, she's in public school." Danielle waved one hand carelessly in the air. "We used to be pretty close, but we don't really have much to say to each other anymore."

"That's too bad," Jack said. "I know what that's like, though. You really have to work at a friendship, otherwise it's easy to drift apart."

Despite her annoyance at the Randall family's appearance, Danielle couldn't help but smile. Jack was trying to make her feel better! It was so sweet—and so insightful and understanding too. It was incredible that he was every bit as handsome as he was nice. Most guys she knew were either one or the other: sensitive nerds or good-looking jerks. Maybe that was just the way it was in high school. But Jack was a college sophomore. Well, it showed.

Danielle smiled irresistibly. Jack was right—you *did* have to work at relationships. And this was one she intended to do just that with. She'd work at it all right . . . very, *very* diligently.

Danielle looked at Jack out of the corner of her eye as she sliced effortlessly through her prime rib. This was one time she couldn't laugh at her mother for using a catering service, she reflected. Not when the food was this impressive. Jack seemed to be enjoying the meal—and the company. She had arranged it so that they could sit right next to each other, and her planning had worked. So far, he'd devoted almost all of his attention to her.

At the other end of the table, Christine seemed interested only in talking to Lori. *Those two have a lot in common*, thought Danielle. Much as she loved her sister, she had to admit that

Christine *was* a bit of a goody-goody. Just like Lori. It was kind of annoying how perfect they both could be.

"Wow, a scholarship," Danielle heard Christine exclaim. "That's terrific, Lori!"

Danielle held back a groan. She hoped her parents wouldn't pick up on the college-application theme. Danielle still hadn't given the matter much thought, and she didn't want Lori showing her up. Not now. Not with Jack here.

"I had no idea you were so interested in fashion design," Christine was going on. "I'd love to see your stuff sometime."

Lori *had* designed a couple of neat outfits, it was true. But Danielle would take a Calvin Klein label over a Randall any day.

"Great!" Lori was beaming. "You should come over if you get a chance. Maybe I could even make something for you," she suggested, shaking pepper onto her baby scallops.

Danielle squirmed in her seat and glanced at Jack as he took a bite out of a dinner roll. She hated it when Lori showed off like this. Besides, Jack wasn't interested in Lori's sewing and knitting. He probably had his own personal tailor!

"I just wish my boss at Tio's Tacos would let me design new uniforms for us workers," Lori went on. "We have to wear these fluorescent orange things. I think he got the idea from staring at the shredded cheese all day long!"

It was just like Lori to bring up the fact that

she served tacos for a living. Danielle rolled her eyes and leaned closer to Jack. "Sorry," she whispered in his ear. "We should be hearing about you, not about chips and salsa."

"You don't need to apologize," Jack assured her with a little laugh. "Christine's told me a lot about all of you—I feel very comfortable just listening."

How tactful! But that was Jack—polite to the last.

"Sounds like you're making a fortune over there, Lor," Christine said jokingly.

A fortune? Give me a break! Danielle practically choked. *More like minimum wage.*

"Not really." Lori blushed. "Actually, I've been saving every penny for college. Your dad started a matching fund for me. For every dollar I save, he'll add a second one."

Danielle's father laughed and lifted his glass of wine in a toast. "Here's to Lori's college fund! Keep up the good work and you'll have enough money to pay for your own college education and Danielle's too. You can bet *she* hasn't been saving anything." He threw his daughter a teasing smile. "Spending is more like it. All you have to do is look at the credit card bills that come in every month."

Danielle's back stiffened, and a red flush crept across her cheeks. Why did her father insist on humiliating her in front of Jack? Danielle had just as much going for her as Lori did—more, probably. But thanks to her father and Christine, Jack was never going to find that out.

Danielle glanced at Jack's profile. He was so handsome and sophisticated! As sexy as Don James was, he wouldn't even make the qualifying round of the race Jack was running. If only there was a way she could see him again . . . she'd show him how right they were for each other.

But after dinner he was going to get into his Mercedes, drive home, and be out of her life forever.

Unless . . . unless Danielle happened to take a trip to visit her sister, who just happened to go to the same school as Jack. After all, Kensington wasn't that far away . . . and neither was Jack Aldrich.

In fact, a convenient excuse for a visit just happened to pop into Danielle's mind. Christine had mentioned some big event at the school coming up soon. Well, Danielle was going to check it out, and *now*! Time was running out!

"Christine," Danielle said, trying to sound casual and offhand. "Isn't next weekend homecoming at Kensington?"

Christine thought for a moment. "Oh, you must mean Junior Weekend."

Danielle took a sip of mineral water. "Junior Weekend?" she asked, feigning innocence. "What's that?"

"It's a chance for high school juniors to visit Kensington," Jack answered. "If they're going to apply for early admissions their senior year, now's a good time to start visiting. There are all kinds of events and interviews set up. A lot of people go. Actually, you might really enjoy it." He looked at Christine. "Don't you think so?"

Danielle wasn't even looking for Christine's reaction. Jack was trying to tell her he wanted to see her again! She looked excitedly at him. "It sounds great. I'd love to come up to Kensington."

Danielle could just see herself walking across campus, Jack at her side. It would be so incredible to spend a weekend on a college campus, on her own, with someone as terrific as Jack.

"Christine looked at several schools before she decided to apply," Danielle's father was saying. "Kids need to test the water before they take the big plunge. Sure, Danielle, it sounds like a good idea."

Danielle broke into a grin. Finally, her dad was helping the situation instead of trashing her. Things were definitely looking good. More than good. It was all going to work out *perfectly*.

"Lori, have you given any thought to Kensington?" Danielle's father was going on. But he didn't wait for an answer. "It's an excellent school. Maybe you could check it out along with Danielle."

All at once Danielle's annoyance was back in full force. What was her father doing? Just horning in on *her* weekend and messing things up. As usual. If Lori came, it wouldn't be the same at all. She'd totally cramp Danielle's style.

In fact, she would ruin everything! Danielle had to do something, and fast.

"But, Daddy, you know Lori isn't interested in a school like Kensington," she pointed out. "She's into fashion—not a high-prestige college education. She wants to go to the Fashion Institute or some other trade school. Right, Lori?"

"Oh, I didn't know that," Mr. Sharp commented. "You're thinking seriously about the Fashion Institute?"

"Well, I really haven't made up my mind," answered Lori. Danielle intercepted her puzzled look. One thing about Lori was that she could always tell when her cousin was up to something. *Read my mind*, Danielle tried to tell her.

"I love designing things, drawing, and sewing," Lori went on to Danielle's annoyance. "It seemed like fashion would be a good thing for me to study."

"Lori, Kensington has a great design program!" Christine interrupted. "At least that's what I've heard."

"Yeah. I have a friend in the program who really loves it," Jack added.

"Why limit yourself before you even get to college?" Christine continued. "Maybe you'll find another area of design in school—an area you like even better than fashion. Maybe you'll end up being an architect!"

Mike Sharp grinned at Christine's comment.

"Now, there's an idea I hadn't thought of," he admitted. Danielle's father always had wanted one of his own daughters to follow in his footsteps and study architecture. Danielle had never been all that interested in it, though—except when he'd been designing Merivale Mall. Now he was looking proudly at Lori as if he were about to offer her a job with his developing company. And all because of Christine's dumb comment. Really! It was too much to take. Danielle didn't even feel like eating the rest of her arugula salad.

"Lori, Kensington is a terrific school," Christine went on. "It's big enough so that there are tons of things to do and all kinds of kids to meet, but it's small enough so that you can make friends and get to know people."

"I guess I'd be a fool not to go and at least look at it," Lori agreed.

"I bet you'd like it there, Lori," said Serena Sharp. Danielle could feel her heart withering up inside—now even her mother was throwing her two cents in!

"You guys could both stay with me," Christine said. "My roommates are going camping for the weekend and I have the whole room to myself!"

"And the air fare's on me, George," Mike Sharp volunteered. "I don't want the girls driving all the way up there. They won't need a car anyway—the campus is small enough to walk anywhere."

"I'm pretty sure I could get off work," Lori said. "And I know we'll have fun." She smiled hopefully at Danielle.

Danielle didn't return her cousin's dopey grin. *Great. Just great.* She ran a nervous hand through her coppery hair. *Now* how was she going to lose Lori for her romantic weekend alone with Jack?

Her father banged his hand on the table. "Then it's settled!" he said. "Even if you don't wind up at Kensington, Lori, it's good to explore your options."

"Well, this is exciting," said Serena Sharp. "I'll call the faculty coordinator tomorrow and tell them to include Lori and Danielle in all the weekend's events!"

Danielle couldn't believe what had just happened. Tonight had to be the worst dinner on record. She just stared, first at her mother and then at her father. The one time in their whole lives they agreed on something, and it had to be this.

Didn't they know they were ruining their daughter's dream weekend? Couldn't they see they were destroying her life?

CHAPTER FOUR

"It's nothing personal, Don. I just don't think we should go out anymore." Danielle spoke in a gentle tone, hoping to soften the blow. With one hand she nervously peeled the label off a bottle of ketchup on the table.

"Nothing personal, huh? You mean it has nothing to do with *me*?" Don James leaned across the table of the booth in O'Burgers and took her hand off the bottle. He threaded his fingers through hers. "I find that kind of hard to believe." Staring at Danielle's hand in his, he shook his head slowly.

"Please don't make this harder than it already is—" Danielle shifted uncomfortably in her seat and slowly tugged her hand free.

"Ah, come on. Give me *some* credit, Red. You're not cutting me loose because you want to. It's those snobby friends of yours coming down on you for hanging out with me," Don said, a catch in his voice. Staring deep into her eyes, he forced her to return his steady gaze.

"Don't be silly," muttered Danielle. He was partly right, of course. But there was so much more to it than that too. She had a college man in her life now, and she would never, ever go back to high school boys again. "It's just—well, we live in two different worlds, that's all," she explained.

"What is this, a soap opera? *You're* rich and *I'm* not. Tell me something I don't know." He placed his forearms on the table and leaned forward, lowering his voice to a conspiratorial whisper. "We were made for each other, and you know it." Don pointed to their reflection in the mirror at the side of the table. "Tell me those two don't belong together."

Danielle had to admit that they did make a great-looking couple. But there was more to a relationship than that—and Jack Aldrich had it all.

Danielle looked away from the mirror. "Listen, Don, I hope we can still be friends—"

"Right," he interrupted. "I know how the rest of that sentence goes. But I know what you *really* mean. You think you're too good for me. Well, okay, but the next time you get lonely, don't come running back to me, because I won't be there."

He paused for a moment, clearly waiting for her to take back what she'd said. It was her last chance, and she knew it. Danielle pressed her eyes shut tight, pushing aside a sudden, surprising ache in her heart. *Good-by, Don*, she thought. Then she opened her eyes.

"So—you ready to go?" Don asked, trying to sound nonchalant. Still, Danielle could hear a faint tremor in his voice. He stood up, casually slinging his leather jacket over one shoulder.

"I can drop you off somewhere if you want," Danielle said, sliding out of the booth and rising to stand beside him. It hurt to look at him, but she forced herself. He had to know that her mind was made up.

Don gave her one last chance. Then he turned and stalked to the cashier's counter, paying the check with a wrinkled ten-dollar bill. Sauntering to the front entrance, he paused and shot Danielle a withering stare.

"Never mind about the ride, I can get home on my own. But I do have one last thing to say, Red, and I'm telling you this as a friend. Your opinion of yourself is getting a little out of hand, and you're going to find that out—the hard way. You think I'm not good enough for you? Okay. Let's see if you can do any better."

Don slipped his muscular arms into his jacket and strolled out of the restaurant, leaving Danielle to stare after him.

For just an instant Danielle had a wild urge to dash after him. Then, as Jack's face filled her imagination, she gave a defiant toss of her magnificent red hair.

Do any better? she thought. *Poor Don. I already have.*

"Remember Mike Bryer, the star running

back at Atwood last year? He goes to Kensington," Nick told Lori on the way to the airport.
"He really likes it there too."

Nick looked at her with a tiny smile, and
Lori tried to return it. But it was no use pretending—they were both upset that she was
going away. Nick and Lori usually spent every
weekend together; with both of them working,
and with Nick's commitments to football and
Lori's to designing, it was often the only time of
the week that they got to see each other. And
now that she'd be gone, they wouldn't be able
to be together for another whole week.

"I hope I have fun," said Lori. "Christine
said we'll get to do everything the students do.
We can use the library, hang out at the student
union—even go to parties." She stared out the
window as they exited the highway.

"Hey," Nick piped up with a nervous laugh.
"Don't have *too* much fun. I don't mind giving
you up for one weekend, but I'd hate for some
Kensington guy to sweep you off your feet while
I'm not around."

"Oh, Nick." Lori laughed. "You know that
would never happen." Quickly, she flipped open
her purse and checked one last time for her
plane ticket. "And besides, I'm going only for
the weekend. Nothing's going to happen in
two days."

Nick pulled up in front of the terminal and
stopped the car. As he turned to face Lori, he
reached across the seat for her hand. "I know.

It's just that I'm so crazy about you—I get scared sometimes."

Lori felt the tips of her fingers tingle with excitement. She knew how much Nick loved her. But even after this long, whenever she heard him say it, it still felt like the very first time. "Nick," she said softly. "Don't worry, okay? You know how much I love you."

Instinctively they leaned toward each other and their lips met in a sweet, passionate kiss. Then they drew apart, and Nick tousled her blond hair affectionately.

"Okay, Randall, I'll let you go. But promise to call me the minute you get home—if not sooner!"

Lori hugged Nick one last time, then slid out of the car, pulling her bags after her. She waved one final good-by as Nick drove away. His kiss lingered on her lips, a sweet reminder. Then she picked up her overnight carry-on bag and portfolio and headed for the ticket counter.

But when she got there, it was only to find that the line curved around the corner. Nervously, Lori glanced at her watch. Only fifteen minutes until flight time. If she waited on that line, she'd miss her plane! Well, it was a good thing she didn't need to check any of her luggage. She had only one bag, plus her portfolio. She could carry all that onto the plane and skip the line completely. All she had to do was find Danielle and then head for the departure gate.

Lori peered down the line of impatient travelers toward the check-in counter. Sure enough, there was Danielle struggling with two stuffed-to-the-max suitcases. Well, it figured. Danielle was notorious for overpacking. Her father had complained one time when she and Lori had been going to summer camp that it would have been easier to bring the camp—horses and all—to Danielle.

"Oh, please let me in," Danielle was begging the middle-aged businessman at the front of the line. "I have to be on a plane in five minutes!"

Lori watched as the man grumbled but let Danielle take his place. Lori had to hand it to her cousin—she knew how to get what she wanted!

Within a few minutes, Danielle's tremendous bags were safely out of the way. "Dani!" Lori called, hurrying over, her bag slung over her shoulder and her portfolio tucked under her arm.

"Oh, hi, Lori," Danielle said, sounding bored.

Lori pressed her lips together. Danielle was always so unenthusiastic around her these days. It was almost hard to believe they'd *ever* been close. But what could she do? She'd tried, but Danielle just hadn't responded—unless, of course, there was something her cousin needed from her.

"Is that all you packed?" Danielle asked, sounding shocked.

Lori shrugged as the two girls hurried off toward Gate Six. "We're going to be at Kensington only until Sunday, right?"

"Yeah, so?" Danielle demanded. "What's your point?"

"Well, um, I guess I just wonder what you're going to do with all the clothes in those suitcases. You couldn't possibly wear all of them in two days."

Danielle sniffed. "I figured I needed a lot of different outfits for, you know, dating and stuff."

Dating and stuff? Lori wondered exactly what Danielle had in mind for one weekend. But then, she'd learned long ago not to try to figure out her cousin. She walked over to the Gate Six counter with Danielle following close behind.

"Hi, I need a boarding pass," Lori told the woman at the desk. "I'd like to sit next to my cousin, if that's all right." She pulled the plane ticket out of her purse and handed it over.

"No problem. Which seat are you in?" the airline representative asked Danielle.

"Sixteen B." Danielle stared uninterested down at one of her perfectly manicured nails as the woman punched Lori's ticket information into the computer. "Hey, Lori, why did you bring that thing?" Danielle asked suddenly, pointing to the portfolio tucked under Lori's arm.

"Uh," Lori hedged. Danielle always made her feel so bad about the things she loved to do—like designing clothing and working at Tio's—that she was almost afraid to tell her cousin the truth. She was hoping the school interviewer would take a look at her work. If that person was anywhere near as impressed as Professor Mortenson from the Fashion Institute had been, it would really help her chances of getting into Kensington. For the weekend Lori had resolved not to think about the fact that her father couldn't afford the tuition. She'd worry about that *after* she got accepted. *If* she got accepted.

"So? What's with the portfolio?" Danielle demanded a second time.

"I have a homework assignment for art class," she lied. It felt bad to do it, but she didn't really have a choice right now. "I need to work on it over the weekend."

Lori was relieved when the flight attendant cut into the uncomfortable conversation. "That's seat sixteen C, and we'll begin boarding in just a few minutes."

"Thank you," Lori said, taking her ticket and boarding pass.

"I should be studying for French, but I'm not going to," Danielle announced as she dropped into a plastic chair facing the window.

"I guess we won't have a lot of time to study, anyway. There's the orientation, the interview, and a tour as soon as we get there," Lori reminded Danielle.

"You're kidding—we have to do all that?"

"It's part of the early-decision process," Lori said, wondering if her cousin had even opened the Junior Weekend pamphlet. "The interview is one of the main reasons they sponsor this weekend at Kensington—so they can screen people early. Do you want to take a look at my pamphlet?"

"No, thanks, I read it. I just forgot about some of the stuff," Danielle said. She stretched her arms over her head and yawned. "I hope it's not as boring as it sounds!" Then she turned her back to Lori, tucking her feet up underneath her, to wait for the plane.

Lori bit her lip. Danielle's message was all too clear—she just wasn't interested in the weekend's events. Or maybe it was *Lori* she found so boring. Lori shook her head, then pulled out her sketch pad. If Danielle wanted to ignore her, there was nothing she could do about it.

An hour later the plane trip was coming to an end. Lori pulled her seat into its upright position and looked out the window as the plane began its descent. For the last hour and a half Danielle had not said one word to her. And there was no sense in trying to start a conversation. The minute they'd sat down, Danielle had pulled a couple of fashion magazines out of her bag and pretty much pretended that Lori didn't even exist. It had been as if she'd put up a big neon sign that said *Lori, Get Lost*. Danielle was like that sometimes.

Lori sighed. It made her sad, but by now

she'd gotten used to it. After Uncle Mike had become successful, Danielle had changed. She didn't seem to need Lori anymore. In fact, she acted almost as if she were embarrassed by her old friend. Lori knew Danielle would come to her if she were ever in trouble, but in their day-to-day lives—in situations that weren't life and death—Danielle was, well, Lori had to say it, snobby.

It was probably from hanging out with all the kids at Atwood. But it still felt awful when Danielle acted as if she didn't care what was going on with Lori—and that seemed to be the case more and more often these days. She just didn't want to talk to Lori—about anything.

Oh, well. Though Lori couldn't pretend it didn't hurt, she also couldn't change things. She pushed the thoughts out of her mind. This weekend was about looking forward, not back. When everything was said and done, Danielle was her cousin, and always would be. And somehow Lori knew that deep down, Danielle did care.

Anyway, that was beside the point right now. As the plane's wheels touched down on the black runway, Lori felt a spark of excitement light up inside her. She was going to spend the weekend at one of the best colleges in the country! It was going to be great! And Lori felt determined. Nothing was going to ruin the next few days for her. Not even Danielle.

CHAPTER FIVE

"I love it!" Lori cried, looking around the Kensington campus as if she was about to burst from excitement. The taxi from the airport had dropped them off right in front of Christine's dorm, and now, after leaving their bags, the two girls were getting their first look at lovely Kensington College.

Silently, Danielle agreed with Lori. The campus *was* beautiful. Ivy leaves covered the old brick buildings. Lush rolling green lawns spread before them like an invitation to stretch out and relax. In fact, that's exactly what a number of students were doing. A few were studying on the grass. Others just sat, chatting with one another.

Danielle's eyes wandered to the huge oak trees that lined the sidewalks. A few students walked past them, kicking the red and yellow autumn leaves that had fallen to the ground.

The place was perfect for her, Danielle decided. It was so New England, and so . . . rich.

"Dani, this is going to be the most fantastic weekend—I can tell." Lori sighed dreamily, her blue eyes shining with enthusiasm.

Lori had put Danielle's own feelings into words. Still, Danielle would never have admitted them. There were people around who might hear—people who'd realize she and Lori were only high school students and didn't *really* belong there.

"This place is all right," Danielle replied casually, "but I hear Princeton is really incredible." If only Lori would stop acting like a tourist!

"That must be the quad." Map in hand, Lori pointed to an open section of the campus bounded by several maples in brilliant red foliage. "The library is over there. That means the student union building must be—"

Danielle couldn't stand it another second. "Lori, do you *have* to carry that map around?" she asked in a harsh whisper. "It makes us look like we've never been on a campus before!"

"We haven't," Lori replied, looking a little amused, which Danielle found *very* annoying. "Anyway, we're going to be late if we don't hurry up and get to the Junior Weekend reception."

Rolling her eyes, Danielle walked briskly into the quad and took a deep breath. Standing on a real college campus, with real college students all around her . . . this was where she belonged. Everyone looked interesting—and sophisticated. Just like Danielle herself.

A totally gorgeous guy hurried by carrying a lacrosse stick. For an instant, his gray eyes met Danielle's green ones, and he tossed her a charming smile. Before Danielle could even return it, he rushed off.

A tiny, satisfied smile pulled at the corners of Danielle's mouth. *This place is full of grade-A hunks*, she thought. *I'm in heaven.* Especially since she'd already met the greatest guy there. John Adams Aldrich the third, also known as Jack . . .

Danielle scanned the quad, absorbing the flavor of the college scene. Jack was probably at his fraternity right now. Maybe even waiting for her. And what was *she* doing? Trudging off to some boring meeting for high school students with Lori! *I bet Jack is dying to show me around*, Danielle thought. *Now all I have to do is ditch Lori and find a phone.*

"Let's see," said Lori, consulting her map again as Danielle shuddered with embarrassment, "the student union building is across from the library—ah! That's it!" she pointed to a huge U-shaped building before them.

Danielle liked what she saw in front of her. Whoever had designed the student union had been smart enough to focus on the real reason anyone went to college—to socialize. A courtyard in front was filled with benches and flower gardens where students could sit and watch people filter in and out of the building. A few couples were sitting with their arms wrapped romantically around each other. The idea that soon she'd be just as close to Jack made Danielle's heart race with excitement.

"We're supposed to go to room two-oh-three," Lori announced, heading toward the union.

Hurrying along the brick paths, Danielle stayed a safe distance behind Lori. She didn't want people to think they were together. On the other hand, she couldn't afford to lose her cousin, who *did* seem to know where they were going. Because if Danielle ever got lost, she would have rather dropped dead than consult a map!

As Lori pushed open the student union's swinging door, Danielle spotted a handwritten sign on the wall. JUNIOR WEEKEND—RECEPTION UPSTAIRS, it said, with an arrow pointing to the blue-carpeted stairs. Thank goodness Lori didn't point that out too. Instead, they just hurried up the stairs and into the reception room.

At the door a bubbly student volunteer handed them each enormous stick-on name tags and a felt-tip marker.

"Forget it," Danielle muttered under her breath as Lori dutifully wrote her name on the tag. "I'm not wearing one of these!" There was no way she was going to stick something to the front of her shirt like a sign, announcing that she was only visiting the college as a high school junior.

Smiling sweetly at the volunteer, Danielle pretended to write her name. Then, turning quickly so that the girl at the door wouldn't notice, Danielle stuffed her name tag into her jacket pocket and surveyed the room. A few Kensington students stood at a long table serving coffee and doughnuts, while others walked around, chatting with the visitors. Another perky volunteer was heading in Danielle's direction.

"Hi, can I help you with anything? Do you have any questions?" the girl asked. Danielle was about to say no, but Lori beat her to an answer.

"Hi, I'm Lori," she said, pointing to the bright red sticker on her sweater. "I'm interested in the design program. Is it part of the art major here, or are they separate?"

"Uh, excuse me," Danielle interrupted. "I'm going to the ladies' room. I'll be right back." Slipping away, she breathed a sigh of relief. Being caught in a room full of all-too-helpful volunteers and high school geeks with name tags on was not her idea of a dream weekend at college!

Danielle walked out into the main corridor and looked around for the bathroom. As a few guys passed, she spotted the boy with the lacrosse stick and smiled. They all smiled back. Danielle suddenly felt on top of the world.

She continued down a few different halls until she spotted a door marked WOMEN. If she could locate the rest rooms in a crowded four-story building without asking for help, she certainly didn't need a map to find the quad, for goodness' sake. And she did *not* need a silly campus tour on an embarrassing bright yellow school bus. What if Jack saw her? It would be humiliating—but just in case it happened, she had to be prepared.

In the bathroom Danielle pulled her velvety teal eyeliner out of her purse and lined her lower lids. The effect of the teal on her green eyes was entirely devastating, and Danielle had to smile. She knew when she was irresistible, and this was one of those times. Jack was going to die when he looked into those baby emeralds.

Having a college man for a boyfriend was going to be fabulous! Teresa and Heather would die of jealousy. Danielle brushed her shimmery red hair one last time and headed back to the reception, casually saying hello to a few students on the way.

The moment she walked into the room she saw him. Jack Aldrich was standing over by the refreshment table talking to a group of visitors. Best of all, Danielle noticed his eyes light up as she hurried across the floor to join him.

"Danielle!" he said, giving her a warm, friendly smile. "It's nice to see you."

As she got closer, Danielle noticed a familiar redheaded figure standing behind Jack—Christine. "Hi there, little sister!" she said enthusiastically. "How's it going?"

Danielle's cheeks reddened. Why did Chris-

tine always have to call her little in front of Jack!
What was she doing here anyway? Trying to
ruin Danielle's entrance? Well, she was suc-
ceeding!

"Welcome to Kensington! Sorry I wasn't in
my room when you got here." Christine gave
Danielle a quick hug. "I had to help my roommates bring their stuff over to the gym—they're
going camping with the Outdoor Club."

"Oh, that's okay." Danielle shrugged. "We
left our bags with the girl next door." Why did
Christine have to act as if she were a baby, as if
she couldn't take care of herself, for heaven's
sake? Especially with Jack standing there, drink-
ing in every word.

"So, Danielle, what have you been doing
all morning?" Jack asked.

Looking for you, Danielle wanted to say. But
of course, she couldn't. Being obvious was not
good strategy for landing the boy of your dreams.
"Not much—actually," she answered. "We came
straight here. I don't even know where Lori is.
Maybe she got lost." *I hope*, Danielle added
silently.

"Oh, I saw her already. We left her over at
the information table, talking to a counselor."
Christine smiled. "I'm really excited that you're
both here."

"Me too," Jack said, nodding at Danielle.

Me three, she said to herself.

"Unfortunately, I have to take off now,"
Jack said, frowning slightly. "I have some re-

search to do for an assignment. I just wanted to make sure you got here okay. I'll see you later—maybe at Sigma!" He waved and headed out the door.

Danielle restrained herself from running out of the room after him. *Just be casual*, she reminded herself. It's okay to be crazy about the guy—you just can't *show* it!

Still, Danielle needed more information. "Isn't Sigma the name of Jack's fraternity?" she asked Christine, trying to sound nonchalant.

"Yeah, Sigma Epsilon Tau. They're having a party tomorrow night. Jack told me to invite you if you're interested."

A zingy feeling went straight through Danielle. Interested? That was putting it mildly. She was ecstatic! Jack had invited her to a party already! Talk about high-gear romances. This one was about to take off at jet speed!

"Uh, excuse me." An annoyingly nasal voice cut through Danielle's thoughts. She turned to find a slightly overweight, bald man walking up behind Christine. "Is your name Danielle Sharp?" he asked her sister. As Christine turned, the man blushed. "Oh, pardon me. I should have recognized you, Christine. I was told Danielle Sharp had red hair, and well . . . I've checked everyone else's name tag but hers."

"Don't worry about it. You're looking for my sister, Professor Tuttle. *This* is Danielle," Christine said graciously. "Danielle, Professor Tuttle."

Danielle stepped up to the professor. "Hello," she said. She didn't really want to talk to this guy, but he was a *teacher*. She could hardly get out of it.

The professor pushed his glasses up on his nose and responded with a wan smile. "My final interview, found at last. I usually wouldn't track a student down, but I'm trying to get to a flute and oboe recital and I thought perhaps we could start our session a little early."

"Oh?" Danielle asked, startled. Lori had mentioned something about an interview—this had to be it. "I mean, oh, of course. No problem."

"Let's see, how about if we find a quiet corner here and have our talk." He looked around distractedly. "How about there?" He pointed to a small table at the far end of the room.

"Good luck," Christine whispered as Danielle followed the professor to a small table at the far end of the room. Settling into a chair, Professor Tuttle consulted his clipboard once more. "Danielle, please have a seat."

"Thank you." Danielle sat down, spreading her pleated miniskirt beneath her.

"I probably don't have to tell you this, but your sister, Christine, is an excellent student."

That's right, you don't have to tell me, Danielle thought, annoyed. *I hear it all the time at home.*

"Now, let's see," the professor continued. "I see that you attend Atwood Academy. Atwood is a fine school, and several good students have come to Kensington from there. I wonder if you'd know any of them?"

"Probably not," Danielle answered with a shrug. She didn't want to tell him she'd been part of the Atwood crowd only for the past couple of years.

"Well, we can't all know everybody, I always say," he chuckled. Then, looking at Danielle with a friendly smile, he asked, "Why don't you tell me why you're here? What do you like about Kensington College?" He pulled a pen from beneath the clip of his clipboard and poised it, eager to write.

Uh-oh. Danielle was freezing up. She knew she had to think of something smart to say. But suddenly her mind was a complete blank. All she could come up with was *I'm here for Jack Aldrich*!

"Don't be nervous, Danielle. This is a very informal interview," Professor Tuttle assured her. He placed his elbows on the table and patiently waited for Danielle to begin.

"Well, I like the campus," Danielle hazarded. "It's very nice—and I like the traditional look. It seems so . . . so *historical* and—uh—well, I know it's a good college—my sister told me all about it." Danielle felt like kicking herself—why hadn't she listened to Lori at the airport?

"I see," the professor noted, writing something down on a sheet of paper. "What field of study do you see yourself pursuing in college?"

Danielle's eyes widened for just an instant

of panic. He wanted to know what she wanted to do with her life. And she couldn't tell him because she didn't know herself! That had always been a problem for her. Her father nagged her about it, her teachers sometimes brought it up. And now this professor had to catch her in it too.

"Let me put it another way." The old professor was trying to sound patient, but Danielle could hear a tinge of annoyance creeping into his tone. "What would you study here at Kensington—assuming you were accepted, of course."

She had to say something. Anything! "Oh! Well—I'm not really sure. I haven't given it a whole lot of thought." She wouldn't get any points with *that* response. If only she could think of something brilliant! Christine would probably have had all the right answers.

"Do you have any questions I could answer about Kensington?"

"Um—I don't think so. It does seem great here, though." Danielle bit her lip and glanced around the room, wishing for an escape. This interview was turning out to be pure torture. If only it would be over, and she could just forget the whole thing had ever happened!

She could see that the meeting wasn't a whole lot of fun for the professor either. "Well," he said, pushing back his chair and standing up. "Maybe you're just a little nervous talking like this in public." He gestured toward the dozens of Junior Weekend participants chatting with students around the room. "If you're serious about applying to Kensington, perhaps you should schedule another interview later on this year." He gave her another wan smile.

"Yes, I'll . . . I'll do that," Danielle said. Then it was official. She'd blown the interview, totally and completely.

"Good-by, Danielle." The professor turned, shaking his head slightly, and left the room.

Oh, who cares, Danielle told herself. *I don't want to come here anyway. I only want to date someone who does.*

But deep down she wasn't feeling quite so flippant. It hurt to be rejected. And this time there was no one she could blame but herself.

Danielle stood in the corridor outside Room 314, waiting for Lori to finish her interview. She tapped her foot impatiently on the carpeted floor. It seemed to be taking hours. Her only consolation for having goofed up her own interview was that she was sure Lori would do exactly the same thing. After all, if a sophisticated girl like herself didn't blow Kensington College off its feet, plain old Lori would never get noticed.

But when the door finally opened and Lori stepped out, Danielle had the sinking sensation that she'd read the situation all wrong. From the ecstatic grin on her cousin's face, she didn't even have to ask how things had gone.

"Danielle," Lori cried, throwing her arms

around her cousin. "He told me I had a good chance of getting in!"

Extracting herself from Lori's embrace, Danielle gulped back disbelief. How had Lori pulled the interview off when she herself had failed so miserably? And the ironic thing was, Lori would never go to Kensington, not in a million years. The Randalls couldn't afford to send her, and that was that.

"And he said there's scholarship money available if I need it," Lori gushed as they headed down to the main floor. "I'm so excited!"

Danielle's green eyes narrowed. It was too much. "Well, hip, hip, hooray," she said dryly. All this reception and interview stuff was getting to be a colossal drag. "When do we get some free time? I want to call some people."

"Well, we have the tour, and then as far as I can tell, we're on our own," Lori said. "We're supposed to meet on the benches in front of the union right about now."

Good, thought Danielle. She couldn't wait to ditch Lori, the Junior Weekend program, and this whole dumb high school scene.

The two cousins strolled out the front door and over to a small cluster of wide-eyed high school students. *What a bunch of nerds*, she thought. After this ridiculous tour she'd have a chance to call Jack.

Maybe he'd ask her to meet him in some romantic out-of-the-way spot on campus. She brightened as she thought about this. Wouldn't it be great to be one of those gorgeous, happy couples strolling across campus . . . kissing under the old clock tower. . . .

"Hello, everyone, and welcome to Kensington College." Danielle's daydream was shattered as the tour guide's voice brought her crashing back to reality. No more clock tower. No more Jack. Just a dozen high schoolers gawking like idiots. "My name is Paul Peterson, and I'll be conducting your campus tour today."

Instinctively, Danielle checked out the tour guide. With his sandy blond hair, bright blue eyes, and straight, freckled nose, he was good-looking—but not nearly as incredible as Jack.

"I hope your interviews went well," he said with a friendly smile as he led them over to a yellow minibus. "Well, here it is—the stretch limousine you requested."

"Home, James," Lori joked. Everyone laughed.

And yet, Danielle wasn't completely sure it was all a joke. Lori's giggle had had a very familiar ring to it—a ring that said, *I'm interested in you*. A ring that spelled pure flirtation . . . maybe Lori hadn't meant it to sound that way, but it hadn't slipped past Danielle.

She peered a little more closely at the tour guide. His bright blue gaze was taking Lori in with more than the normal amount of attention. So he liked her too. . . . Danielle smiled wickedly. Maybe a little romance was igniting for Lori. And with Nick Hobart waiting impatiently back home, that meant fireworks.

Hmmm, Danielle thought. *Looks like Lori's perfect Junior Weekend is taking a turn toward trouble.* She couldn't help feeling just a twinge of satisfaction. Now she just had to make sure her own weekend ended up perfectly—in Jack Aldrich's arms.

CHAPTER SIX

Lori slid across the beige vinyl seat and stared out the window of the bus, trying to get unflustered. She hadn't meant to make that joke—it had just slipped out, and suddenly she was the center of attention.

But that wasn't all. What was really making her pulse pound was that gorgeous tour guide! She couldn't mistake the way his eyes kept seeking hers out, or those gentle, leading smiles he was throwing her way. He had definitely noticed her. And Lori had to admit to herself that she liked being noticed by him.

"Just a little background about Kensington before we start out," Paul said, smiling again at Lori. "Kensington College was founded in 1823. On the left you can see the dean's house, which was the first building on campus."

Paul faced the students with his back to the dashboard as the driver revved the engine and pulled out. His voice sounded clear and gentle over the microphone. Lori listened carefully, at the same time trying not to stare at him. But it was hard to ignore him. His deep blue eyes radiated warmth and intelligence. Lori could practically feel the silkiness of his sandy blond hair as he raked his long fingers through it.

"On your right you'll see North Hall. Before this dorm was built, cows used to graze out here. I guess students were a little reluctant to move in at first, due to the aromatic cow fragrance in the basement. . . ."

Everyone on the bus laughed, and Lori couldn't help joining in. Paul was friendly, smart, funny, cute—

Cut it out, Lori warned herself. *You've already got the greatest boyfriend ever!*

But Paul's eyes seemed to search Lori out, and she couldn't help blushing. Something in his clear blue gaze made her feel as if he were looking right into her thoughts. She squirmed a little in her seat and twisted a strand of her blond hair around her finger. *It's like he can read my mind. And if he can*, she mused, *he knows I'm attracted to him.*

Nervously, she scanned the bus for Danielle, who'd inched her way to the back. If there were ever a time she needed her cousin to distract her, this was it. But Danielle was looking at her nails, as if the campus tour were more boring than a date with Keith Canfield, Atwood's number-one bug collector. She didn't even notice Lori gazing at her desperately.

"Over to our right is the fine arts building. You've probably heard about Kensington's programs in design, painting, and sculpture—they're known for being the best among small colleges. I spend a lot time in that place," Paul commented, looking at Lori and smiling.

He's interested in art and design too, Lori thought. *Just like me.* She started to smile back at him, then bit her lip and gazed out the window again. This was just too weird. No one but Nick had ever had this kind of effect on her. Of course, no one but Nick was half as good-looking as Paul—

Lori's eyes widened as she realized the direction her thoughts were going. *Pull yourself together,* she advised herself sternly. *And stop looking at him!*

Still, no matter how hard she tried to avoid it, her gaze kept drifting back to Paul's handsome, tanned face. Each time he was staring right back at her. And she just couldn't ignore the tingle of excitement that was building inside her.

Too soon, the van pulled up in front of the student union. Lori tried to tell herself she was relieved. The tour was over, and she'd never see Paul again—and that was probably for the best.

She stood up and waited to get off the bus. But as she stepped down the last stair, her knees suddenly buckled and she felt herself falling.

Paul, who was standing by the door, caught Lori in his strong arms and kept her from tumbling to the ground. As he pulled her to her feet, his gaze locked with hers. She couldn't help noticing that the blue in his eyes was flecked with tiny dots of gold. Suddenly she was breathless. His arms felt so good around her!

"Watch your step, Lori," he said, gradually letting her go although he didn't seem to want to.

"I'm fine. I'm sorry. Um, thanks!" Lori's voice sounded silly and awkward to her, as if she'd never talked to a boy before. "How did you know my name?" she asked.

"Mental telepathy," he said gravely. For a moment Lori was startled. Then he winked. "That and the name tag."

"Oh!" Lori gasped. "Of course!"

"Your legs were probably asleep from sitting so long—and listening to me go on and on about Kensington," he joked. "Well," he said, brushing his hair back from his forehead. "Have a nice weekend, Lori. Maybe I'll see you around."

"Yeah, maybe—" Lori mumbled. She couldn't think of anything else to say. Paul flashed her a grin, then turned and strode easily away.

I'm a real genius today, Lori thought ruefully. *First I fall over my feet, then I trip over my tongue—he's never going to want to see me again!*

Then she caught herself. Did she really want to see Paul again? Suddenly she felt a little frightened. She'd promised Nick that no Kensington guy would sweep her off her feet—but hadn't Paul almost done just that?

"I warn you, the food isn't from Premier Caterers," said Christine with a giggle. She grabbed a tray and a set of silverware, then started down the cafeteria line. Danielle and Lori trailed after her, pushing their own trays along. "Yuck!" Christine commented as she stared into a pan labeled tuna surprise. "That stuff's the worst. I think it's time to break out my Care package from home. Mom sent me some Belgian chocolates, Danielle. They're so rich I've been saving them for a special occasion, and guess what? You're it!"

It's funny that Mom had time to send Christine chocolates, Danielle thought, jealousy creeping into her mind. *She never does anything nice like that for me!*

"Tonight's buffet night, so you guys should just help yourselves," Christine said as they pushed their trays along the metal rack. "Now, the tuna surprise is poisonous, but the chicken cacciatore is usually pretty good—as long as it was made today."

Following Christine's suggestion, Danielle reached for the serving spoon and dumped a helping of the steaming cacciatore onto her green plastic plate. "At least it's hot, that's a good sign," she told Lori, who helped herself too.

"There's Jack!" Christine exclaimed just as the girls headed for the soda machine. Danielle whipped around, craning her neck to see where he was. Aha!

He was on his feet waving and calling out her name! "Come on over here!" he shouted, cupping his hands in a makeshift megaphone.

"Oh, hey, Jack!" Danielle called back. Excited, she turned to Lori and Christine. "Look, will you guys get me a diet Coke? I'm going to sit with Jack." Without waiting for an answer, she threaded her way between tables and across the crowded dining hall.

"There you are!" Jack said when Danielle finally made it. He looked fantastic in his mossy green cashmere sweater; it had probably cost as much as an airplane ticket to Europe. Danielle watched him intently as she placed her tray on the table—so intently that her cacciatore almost landed in her tapioca pudding. Luckily for her, Jack had been gazing into her eyes and not at her plate. She gave him her famous thousand-watt smile and sat down next to him.

"So, Danielle, are you enjoying your visit?" Jack asked. He seemed so pleased to see her that Danielle wondered if he wasn't going to kiss her right then and there. But he didn't. *Too bad*, she thought with a secret smile.

She watched as Jack motioned to Lori and Christine to join them. "Here—there are enough seats for all of us," he said, grabbing an empty chair from another table.

Oh, why did he have to be so polite, Danielle wondered. It was a nice trait, but now

Lori and Christine were going to be with them for the whole dinner. What a drag.

"Hi, Jack!" said Lori, sliding into the seat across from Danielle.

Christine lowered her tray across from Jack. "Hi! Here's your soda, Dani. By the way, Jack, I have that book you lent me." She pulled a paperback from her bag and gave it to him.

"You can keep it if you need it," he offered.

"Thanks," answered Christine, "but I have too many other things on my mind. Would you believe I have to turn in a thirty-page paper on the Industrial Revolution on Monday and I have a statistics test on Tuesday?"

"I believe it," Jack said. He took a blue knapsack off the back of his chair and unzipped a pocket. "Guess who just came from the library?" He stuffed the book into the already full knapsack and hooked the strap back onto his chair. "See, girls, life at Kensington isn't all fun and games. That's why we have to *schedule* our parties. Otherwise people would never know when to stop studying and start relaxing."

"Oh, Jack, you're so funny!" Danielle cooed. "It can't be that bad, can it?" She played with her fork. The last thing she wanted to do was eat a plateful of chicken in tomato sauce while Jack was staring at her. If she'd been thinking straight, she would have picked out something a lot less messy, like melba toast and soup. But there were Lori and Christine, eating bite after bite of the cacciatore. Obviously, they didn't care *what* they looked like.

Jack took a sip of his chocolate milk. "I hope you're all coming to the Sigma party tomorrow night. The guys have been getting ready for it all week, and I told them you might be there." He gave Christine a significant look.

Has he been talking to Christine about me, Danielle wondered as she saw it. *He must really like me!* Her heart sang. "I'll be there," she promised.

Lori frowned. "I don't know," she said. "Maybe I'll come for an hour or so. I've got some homework I might have to do Saturday night!"

Danielle knew that was a half truth; Lori was worried about something or other—Danielle suspected it had to do with "the tantalizing tour guide"—and seemed ready to hibernate for the rest of the weekend. That was fine with Danielle. The more time alone with Jack, the better!

"Any chance you can make it, Christine?" Jack asked. Danielle could tell from the tiny concerned crease of Jack's forehead that he was worried she would say yes. But he had to invite Christine, it was the polite thing to do.

Thankfully, Christine seemed reluctant to commit herself. "Jack, you know I'd love to come, and if I finish my paper, I will. But I don't think I'm going to be done until really late."

Good! Danielle thought. Tomorrow she'd be alone with Jack!

But wait—that would already be Saturday night—and Saturday was way too late. By noon Sunday she would be on the plane home!

"Well, what do you all do here on *Friday* nights?" she asked. She opened her green eyes wide and attempted to look innocent. "I mean, are there any extracurricular activities?"

"A couple," said Jack between bites of his chocolate cake. "There's a free movie tonight, actually."

"Really?" cooed Danielle. "What movie?"

"Oh, I doubt it's anything you'd be interested in. I think it's called *The Blender*. The psych department is sponsoring it."

"What's that? It sounds like a horror flick!" Danielle shivered, hoping that Jack would offer to go with her and hold her hand.

"Yeah, it's one of those really gross, scary movies. Rated R for 'revolting.' "

Jack is so much fun! I'll bet he thinks Christine is pretty boring—all she ever wants to do is study.

"Well, a movie is out for me," Christine threw in, as if on cue. "I've got to work."

"Revolting, huh? I love scary movies. But I hate going to them alone," Danielle hinted. "I get soooo nervous!"

"Gosh, Danielle, I wish I could go with you." Christine looked sincerely worried. "I hate for you to be alone on your first night here."

"Well," Jack volunteered, "I'm pretty well

caught up on my work. Actually, I was just going to hang out tonight. Want me to go with you, Danielle?"

Danielle's eyes lit up. *All right!* At last she'd be alone with him, and in a darkened theater too. And later they could go out to someplace with a piano and candlelit tables. And then he'd drive her back to campus in his blue Mercedes and everyone would see them. Danielle could practically feel his arm around her. And when the evening was over he'd tell her what a fantastic person she was, and come closer for a lingering good-night kiss. . . .

"How about you, Lori? Feel like getting terrified for free tonight?" Jack asked.

Lori laughed. "Okay, sure. I'll give it a try," she agreed. "As long as you'll be there to protect us from the blender."

Danielle forced a bite of chicken down her throat to keep herself from screaming. Lori had some nerve to go to the movie when it was obvious that she'd be a third wheel. Really, that girl had *no* brain sometimes. How she'd managed to impress her interviewer, Danielle had no idea.

"Great!" said Jack. "Then I'll meet you both in front of the student union at seven forty-five. I'd better take off now, though. If I'm going to a movie tonight, I have to do some reading first. Enjoy the rest of your dinner. Try the cake, it's almost good!"

"Bye, Jack!" said Christine. "And thanks for entertaining Danielle and Lori."

Danielle could have killed Christine. Jack was her date, not her baby sitter. Why did Christine always have to treat her like a seven-year-old?

Jack stood up and grabbed his leather jacket from the back of his chair. "*Ciao*, girls!" he called as he began to weave his way around the tables toward the exit.

"See you later, Jack!" Throwing him a sweet smile, Danielle waited until he had walked out the front door. Then she tossed her fork onto the tray with a frown. "I'm going to go get ready," she announced. "I'll see you back at the room."

Danielle didn't bother to bus her tray. Instead, she stormed right out the front door, holding her head high in the air.

How dare Lori come along on *her* date with Jack Aldrich! Well, one thing was for sure—she was going to have to find a way to get rid of Cousin Lori tonight—one way or another.

CHAPTER SEVEN

Danielle scanned the crowd milling in front of the psychology building. As she wandered around the terrace, she hoped Jack was already there, watching her. She had spent a good hour and a half deciding what to wear, and now she was a little late, but so what? Her ensemble was designed to knock Jack off his feet. Stonewashed jeans hugged her hips and accentuated her long legs, and she had on one of her favorite Norwegian ski sweaters, the one with the blue and green pattern that matched her eyes.

She had tried to get that casual yet put-together college look—and she knew she had succeeded by the way all the guys outside the building were staring at her. They were obviously wondering who the new gorgeous girl on campus was, and how they could possibly meet her.

Lori had gone for a walk, giving Danielle the opportunity to make a solo entrance, and

Danielle was relieved that she was meeting Lori here, outside, and in the dark. *I'm beginning to feel like we're attached at the hip!*

But Danielle wasn't really interested in getting to know any of those guys who were checking her out—she wanted only to see Jack. Where was he?

She flipped her auburn hair over her shoulder and turned to look in the other direction. But as she moved forward, she found her way blocked by a broad masculine chest—a chest in a green cashmere sweater and a leather jacket. Jack!

Throwing him one of her brightest smiles, Danielle said, "Well, hello there."

"Greetings, Danielle," he responded suavely, laughing in a way that sent a shiver through her body. "I was about to give up on you."

"I hope I'm not too late." She pouted prettily. "Have you been waiting long?"

"Mmm . . . sort of. I think we'll be lucky if we get seats. The psych department did a good job advertising this movie."

Danielle looked at the steady stream of Kensington students filing into the building. It didn't say much for the social life when the entire campus population turned out for a B movie.

Well, at least Lori hadn't shown up yet. Maybe she'd gotten lost on her walk—she probably couldn't see her map now that it was dark outside.

Suddenly, Jack stood on his tiptoes to see

over the crowd and called out, "Lori, we're over here! She was trying to find you," he explained to Danielle.

Oh, great. Danielle rolled her eyes. *So much for a romantic evening.* As Lori edged her way around the crowd toward them, Danielle couldn't believe her eyes. Lori was actually wearing her red and black Merivale High jacket. She brought one bag, and she had to put this in it? Danielle shook her head. Why didn't Lori just make an announcement over the public address system —"Hi, I'm in high school!"

"There you are, Dani! We were looking all over for you," said Lori with a friendly grin.

"Mm-hmmm! Here I am!" Danielle said lightly. "And there *you* are!" *Unfortunately, we're both in the same place,* she added to herself.

"Okay, now that we're all here, let's go in," Jack suggested. The line had all but disappeared, and only a few other people walked in the door ahead of them.

As Danielle looked around the packed auditorium, she couldn't help breaking into a smile. There was no way they were going to find three seats together. She did see a few doubles, however. People seemed to be sitting in large groups just like in the dining hall, talking and calling out to friends several rows away.

Jack waved to a bunch of guys in the second to last row. "Standing room only," he observed. "Why don't you two hurry and find seats together? I can sit by myself."

"Don't be silly!" Danielle countered. Quickly spotting two seats in the sixth row down, she cried, "There are two right there, Jack!" With a not-so-gentle tug, she grabbed his arm and pulled him down the first step. "Lori doesn't mind sitting by herself—do you, Lori?"

By the look on Lori's face, Danielle could see a light bulb going off in her head. *At last, she's getting the picture*, thought Danielle thankfully. She threw a smile in her cousin's direction. *Lori knows what it's like to be in love. I'm sure she'll leave us alone now that she realizes what's going on.*

"I don't mind," Lori said. "See you guys later." She smiled at them before turning to walk down the steps of the auditorium.

"Thanks, Lori. You're a doll!" Danielle yelled over all the conversations around them. Good old Lori. She always did come through at the last second. Danielle tugged at Jack's hand pulling him down the stairs and in the direction of the two empty seats she'd located.

"Sorry—" She shrugged, and smiled. "I saw a couple of people about to grab our seats, and I thought we'd better hurry."

Jack nodded and smiled but didn't say anything. *Good*, thought Danielle, excited. *He didn't argue with me. That proves he's secretly glad Lori's gone.*

All she had to do now was make herself comfortable and wait for the lights to go down.

* * *

Lori continued down to the front of the room, feeling a little conspicuous for being all alone.

She also felt a little foolish. She should have known Danielle was interested in Jack Aldrich. After all, he was handsome and rich, the two characteristics Danielle valued most in a guy. It was weird, though: Lori had gotten the impression that Jack was kind of interested in *Christine*. . . . Maybe not, though.

Anyway, Lori decided, after the awful way Danielle had been treating her lately, she'd rather not sit with her. She might end up with a sore neck sitting in the front row, but it was a whole lot better than a bruised ego.

In the very front row, off to the far side, Lori thought she saw a couple of empty seats. She slowly made her way through the row, being careful not to step on anyone's toes.

"Excuse me, is anyone sitting there?" she asked a nice-looking blond girl who was talking to the guy next to her.

"The one against the wall is free," the girl replied, looking up at Lori. "We're saving this one for a friend." She patted the seat next to her.

Lori sat down next to the wall. It felt weird to be at a movie without Nick. Who would she hold on to when she was afraid? She missed having his arm around her and snuggling up close, leaning her head on his shoulder. She'd been away from him for only a day, but it seemed like forever.

The lights began to dim, and the last few stragglers rushed for the remaining seats.

"Paul—over here!" the blond girl called to a figure standing in the shadows of the aisle.

Lori looked up and froze. Just hearing that name made her stomach do a flip-flop. There were probably ten Pauls at Kensington; it couldn't be the *same* Paul she'd met that afternoon.

But it was! And he was stepping over people's feet to reach the seat next to hers.

"Is that Lori, the girl with the name tag?" he asked as he unfolded his seat. "Are you here all alone?"

"Um, yes," she answered, glad the lights were lowered and he couldn't see her blush.

"I hope your legs don't fall asleep again. But from what I hear about this movie, I'm sure it won't be as boring as my tour!"

"Oh, I wasn't bored—it was just the traveling and all," Lori said quickly. She felt an idiotic grin unfold across her face and she wanted to kick herself. Why couldn't she act like a human being around Paul? Why did he make her feel so dizzy and unsure of herself?

Lori squeezed her eyes shut and tried to calm down.

"Hey, don't close your eyes now. Save that for the scary parts!" Paul whispered.

Lori's eyes flew open and she smiled at him. "Um, I was only practicing."

"Gee, I hope this movie isn't too awful,"

Danielle whispered into Jack's ear as she clutched his arm with both hands. "Actually, I love old movies—you know, the classics. They're so *romantic*. Greta Garbo is my favorite actress." Maybe she could impress Jack with her good taste. "Of course, with *you* here, I won't be afraid at all." She leaned closer.

Soon after the movie started, and the scary music began building to an ominous crescendo, Danielle let out a tiny shriek of terror. With that out of the way, she edged closer and closer to Jack in her seat. When the psychotic in the movie turned the blender speed up to purée, Danielle buried her face in Jack's sleeve and caressed his bicep. "I can't look!" she squealed, her voice muffled by his soft sweater.

Jack seemed engrossed by the movie. And he kept shifting around, as if his chair were uncomfortable. *Maybe he has a backache*, Danielle thought. *He's probably tense from all that studying. What he needs is a massage.*

Danielle wished Jack would put his arm around her, or at least hold her hand. But it was obvious that all those hours at the library had taken their toll. Jack was too exhausted to do anything but stare straight ahead at a movie about an appliance. Oh, well. If he rested now, at least he'd be ready to dance the night away tomorrow at the Sigma party.

With that thought, Danielle grabbed Jack's hand. Clutching it firmly, she settled back to enjoy the rest of the movie.

*   *   *

"I never loved you, you fool! It was a—"

Suddenly the grating music stopped and the screen went blank. A disappointed groan went up from the crowd as the overhead lights came on in the auditorium. "I want my tuition money back!" somebody yelled, sending a ripple of laughter around the room.

Lori turned around and looked up at the projection room. If the movie didn't start playing soon, she was going to have to talk to Paul. Couldn't they fix the problem right away?

"Well," said Paul, smiling easily at Lori. "Just when it was getting interesting too." He patted his mouth, pretending to yawn, then let out a little laugh.

Lori laughed too. Suddenly she decided she really wanted him to like her. *Loosen up, Lori,* she said to herself. *It's no big deal just talking to the guy.* But her body only tensed up more.

"Honestly," he went on, "sitting here in silence is a lot more fun than watching a crazy person wipe out his family, isn't it?"

Lori felt her face turn red. "I guess so," she mumbled.

"How are you enjoying life on campus? Do you think you might like it here—if they get new projectors, that is?"

Smiling, Lori said, "I think I could get used to it. But it's a little overwhelming at first."

He nodded understandingly, staring back into her eyes with that hypnotic gaze of his. "I know what you mean," he said. "I remember how I felt on *my* Junior Weekend. Kind of like you're on the outside looking in, right?"

"Kind of *exactly* like that," Lori agreed. Paul had a wonderful way of putting things.

All of a sudden the loudspeaker let out a huge earsplitting whine. Several boos echoed throughout the auditorium. "Sorry, everybody," a girl's harried voice announced, "but *The Blender* has, ah, eaten the rest of the film. I guess you'll all just have to imagine the ending. Sorry again, but we're disconnecting it for the night."

Well. Lori's heart beat faster. She had two options: she could go find Danielle and Jack—or she could strike up a conversation with Paul.

Or she could leave. But if she were really honest with herself, she'd have to admit that she really didn't *want* to leave. And, anyway, with Paul's long legs stretched out in front of him, it would be too embarrassing to crawl over him, especially after practically falling off the bus that afternoon. He'd think she was such a klutz!

Well, all she'd have to do was talk with him for a minute or two, and then, when people started leaving, she could make her getaway. After that she'd never have to face the guy again. When the weekend was over, she'd go back to Merivale and Nick and forget all about Paul. . . .

And yet she couldn't deny the twinge of disappointment that had sneaked into her heart at the thought. Never to see Paul again . . .

never to feel that forbidden thrill again . . . was that what she really wanted?

Lori just didn't know anymore, but she figured it was better to be safe than sorry.

"Well," she said, "I guess I'd better get back to the dorm. My cousin Christine is probably waiting for me."

"You're going to meet up with her now?" Paul asked, frowning slightly. "Too bad. I hope I'll see you again before you go home, Lori."

"Well, I'll be pretty busy, actually. Good night!" And without lingering a second longer than she had to, Lori stepped over Paul's legs and walked along the row of seats until she reached the aisle. She climbed the steps up to the exit, then paused for a moment to look back over the auditorium.

Lori saw a sign just outside the door to the lecture hall: SEATING CAPACITY: 400.

Four hundred people in there, and I end up sitting next to Paul. Pretty incredible odds!

CHAPTER EIGHT

Please let it be before nine o'clock, Danielle thought as she pushed open the glass door to the dining hall. If she missed breakfast, she'd also miss an opportunity to see Jack.

Picking up a tray, Danielle looked around the huge room. It wasn't nearly as crowded as it had been the night before—in fact it was practically deserted. A few students seemed to be lingering over coffee, talking or reading. Danielle wondered if people at Kensington ever did anything *but* study. Jack included. There was no sign of the gorgeous Aldrich heir.

"Danielle, over here!" a familiar voice called. Christine was standing up and waving to her with Lori sitting beside her.

Since the eggs looked about two hours old, Danielle picked up some cold cereal, some juice, and a cup of tea.

She strolled casually over to Christine. "Why

didn't you wake me up?" she asked, irritated. "I told you I wanted to get up early."

"We tried," Christine replied with a smile. "You told us to get lost! And as I recall, the last time I woke you up early you made me swear never to do it again!"

Her sister had a point. When they were living at home together, Christine had always been the early bird in the family. Once when they were really little, Christine had tried to wake up Danielle at the crack of dawn, and Danielle had thrown all her stuffed animals at her sister, one after the other.

"Have you seen Jack?" Danielle asked, trying to act nonchalant. "I don't see him anywhere."

After the movie, he'd just walked her back to the dorm and said something about getting up early the next morning. No good-night kiss or anything! Well, at least they had both gotten a good night's sleep, Danielle consoled herself. And Jack would be ready for their date *that* night anyway—even if he'd practically sleepwalked through the last one.

"No, I haven't seen him. Have you, Lori?" Christine asked. "Lori got here before me."

"He was just leaving when I showed up," Lori said.

"Where was he going?" Danielle wanted to know.

"I don't know, I didn't ask him," Lori answered with a shrug. "We just waved hello."

She looked at her cousin as if she wished she could help.

Danielle smiled weakly at her, then took a sip of her tea.

"I wish I could spend some time with you this afternoon, but that paper is still hanging over my head," Christine said. "I've just got to get it done. Do you think you can manage on your own?"

"Sure!" said Lori. "I thought I'd check out the bookstore and take another long walk around campus. It really helped me get a feel for the place."

Thank goodness! Lori wouldn't be following her around all day. And Christine would be busy too. That meant Danielle could take her own walk—to wherever Jack was. Maybe he'd be in his room on a Saturday morning.

"Do guys spend a lot of time at their fraternity houses on weekends?" Danielle asked Christine.

"Well, some do, some don't," she replied. "A lot of them are on sports teams, so they have games today. Why? Did you meet someone new and interesting last night?" Christine's azure eyes twinkled mischievously.

Lori was looking at her too, as if she were waiting for Danielle to tell them what had happened between her and Jack.

"No, I didn't," Danielle huffed. "I was just wondering."

"Sorry," Christine said. "You'll definitely meet a lot of guys tonight." Christine turned to

Lori. "Are you sure *you* can't go to the Sigma party tonight, Lor? They usually have the best parties on campus."

Lori grimaced and put down her coffee cup. The idea of going to a party seemed to have turned her stomach. "I'd like to, but I can't. I've got work to do."

"Oh, Lori, that's too bad," purred Danielle, secretly thrilled that Lori wouldn't be at her side to tell everyone that they were high school juniors. She thought she knew the real reason Lori wanted to stay in—Lori was afraid of running into that tour guide yet again.

"Well, I don't really think I should go either, Lori," Christine admitted. "I should spend tonight working my paper. Looks like you'll have to have enough fun for the three of us, Danielle."

No problem, Danielle said to herself.

Christine reached for her tray and stood up. "I'm off to study. See you later!"

After they watched Christine's lithe figure walk away, Lori and Danielle sat in an awkward silence while Danielle finished her tea. "Well, I guess I'll get going now too," Lori finally said. "Have fun today, Danielle."

Danielle nodded blankly at her cousin. "You too," she murmured, her mind racing ahead to the next part of her plan.

When her cousin was out of sight, Danielle pushed aside her tray, stood up, and walked over to a red phone located just inside the entrance. It looked like a campus extension, so Danielle picked up the receiver and dialed O, hoping to reach the switchboard.

"Operator. Can I help you?"

"Yes, could you connect me to the Sigma Epsilon house, please?" Danielle asked politely.

Danielle listened to the phone ring eight or nine times, then lost count. "Sigma!" a deep voice yelled into Danielle's ear just as she was about to give up.

"Oh, hi," she said cheerily. "Is Jack Aldrich there?"

"Hold on a second. Jack! Aldrich!" the guy shouted. It sounded like the party had already started. There was so much noise at the other end of the phone that Danielle wondered if it could really be nine-fifteen on a Saturday morning. The guy who'd answered must have dropped the phone on the floor, as a loud crashing came through the line. Danielle jumped.

"Sorry about that," he said when he got back on the phone. "Look, Jack's not around. Somebody said he's probably at the library. Who, or is that *whom*, shall I say was calling?" he asked.

"Danielle—Danielle Sharp," she said.

"Well, Danielle, will I see you at our party tonight?"

"You sure will," Danielle responded with a little laugh. *I'll be the one with Jack Aldrich.* "Thanks for your help," she added, and hung up.

If Danielle remembered correctly, the library

wasn't too far from the cafeteria. She rummaged in her purse for her lipstick and a small mirror. She carefully applied a fresh coat of red and ruffled her coppery hair with her fingers to give it more body. She'd get Jack away from his books in no time!

Wow! thought Lori as she browsed through the student bookstore. *This place goes on forever!*

She couldn't decide which section to check out first, but she had a feeling it should be fashion. She wanted to look at the books professors used for some of the courses. Maybe she could even buy one.

Stopping in front of the shelves with the heading DESIGN, ETC., she picked up a large red volume titled *A Complete History of Fashion*.

The book contained color illustrations of clothes from several different periods. Lori leafed through it slowly, savoring each page—she could have sat right down on the floor and spent the rest of the day just looking at it.

Turning the book over to check the price, Lori winced. It would take almost all her spending money. Still, this wasn't a book she could find at home, and it was an investment in her future. . . .

"Don't buy it."

A male voice directly behind Lori startled her. Spinning around, she found herself looking into that unmistakable pair of gorgeous blue eyes once again.

"Paul! Hi!" Lori looked down at her feet awkwardly. After that stupid way she'd acted at the movie the night before, she thought he'd never speak to her again.

Nevertheless, there he was, standing right next to her and grinning at her. *Christine told me this was a small campus, but this is ridiculous*, Lori thought.

"I'm buying a really fascinating book." Paul laughed and held up a copy of *Adventures in Biotechnological Software*. "Mine happens to be required reading, but you don't *have* to buy that one. So don't."

Lori glanced at the book in her hands. "Why not?" she asked. "It looks fantastic."

"It is. However, you can have it on indefinite loan from a friend—me. It was one of the texts in a design class I took last semester, and I don't really need it anymore. I held on to it because I liked the pictures so much."

"And you're not still taking design courses?"

"Actually, I have two this semester. I'm a design major," he said, laughing.

"You're kidding! That's what I want to study in college!" Lori exclaimed.

"Well, would you like to meet the author of that book?" Paul asked. "He's the department chairman, and he also happens to be my adviser. Come on—it'll be a lot more interesting than hanging out in the bookstore. I promise. Besides, he's always got his eye out for new, talented students."

"Oh, I don't know how talented I am. I wish I had my portfolio with me, though. It's back in my cousin's dorm."

"We can pick it up on the way. That'll give us more time to talk," Paul said, taking the book out of Lori's hands and putting it back on the shelf. "Don't worry, I'll still lend you my copy," he promised.

More time to talk! He wanted to get to know her! How fabulous—that is, how terrible! Lori didn't know how she felt about it except that it was driving her crazy.

"Okay, I guess—I mean—sure! Let's go!" The chance to meet a professor of design was something Lori couldn't pass up. After all, that was why she was at Kensington—to explore the college.

Now, if only her hands would stop shaking and her heart would stop pounding every time she looked at Paul . . .

CHAPTER NINE

Danielle rarely forced herself to enter a library. Reading wasn't one of her favorite pastimes—why read about it when you can live it? was her opinion. But if Jack liked books, Danielle could tolerate the library for a few hours. He was in there somewhere, and she was going to find him if she had to look behind every dusty, musty, old stack.

Luckily for her, Jack was sitting at a long oak table in the reference room—alone except for the small tower of books in front of him. *Now*, thought Danielle as she walked softly toward him. *How can I make this look natural?*

"Good morning, Jack!" she said in a loud stage whisper.

"Hi, Danielle," he replied, glancing up from his book with a quizzical expression. "What brings you to the library?"

"Well"—Danielle paused—"I'm working on an important term paper, and I thought I'd do a little research here. This library makes the one at Atwood look pathetic." *And you make the guys at Atwood look pathetic too!*

"What subject are you working on?"

Danielle stole a quick glance at the books on the table. "Psychology," she said casually.

"That's funny, so am I."

"No kidding? What's your paper about?"

"Oh, it's about siblings, actually, and how birth order affects their personalities."

"You mean, like Christine and me? We are incredibly different, you know," Danielle said, giving Jack her sexiest look.

"Uh—yes, I bet you are. Maybe you could give me some examples."

"Well, sure. Let's see, Christine is a very serious person. Her room is always neat, she studies a lot. But me, well, I think I like a more exciting life—that's it, I'm more spontaneous. Christine likes to plan everything to death," Danielle said, looking at Jack. "I live for the moment." Danielle waited for Jack to agree with her.

He was silent. Danielle realized he'd need a little more prodding. "Feel like taking a break? We can go for a walk or something."

"No, I can't. I've still got too much to do. But I'll see you tonight at the party, right?"

"Of course I'll be there! That's one plan I don't mind keeping," she joked.

"Good. I'm looking forward to it." Jack

smiled back at her, opened his book, and began to read.

Momentarily flustered, Danielle hung her coat on the end of a bookshelf and meandered down the aisle, glancing at a few books. Every now and then she sneaked a sidelong glance at Jack. He looked irresistible when he was concentrating.

In fact, he was so irresistible that Danielle couldn't help herself. She strolled back to his table.

"Guess what? I just saw the neatest book," she whispered in his ear. It was called *Courtship and Trauma in Transylvania*. Can you imagine?" She giggled, pulled out the chair next to Jack, and sat down. Leaning closer, she put her hand on the back of his chair, and asked, "What's that you're reading? *Territorial Behavior Among Siblings*. Sounds fascinating!"

Jack rubbed the bridge of his nose. "Um, I really don't know," he mumbled. "I haven't had a chance to read it yet. And if I don't, I'm going to flunk my test in class on Monday. So I'll talk to you later, okay?"

With that, he buried his face in the book again. Danielle stared at the back of his handsome head. Could he really prefer some old book to *her*? There was no way.

She'd have to try something else to draw him out of his shell. And if anyone could figure out how, Danielle Sharp could.

* * *

Lori stared anxiously out the window behind the design professor's desk and tried to prepare herself for his criticism. He'd been looking through her portfolio for the last five minutes without saying a word. Lori would be just crushed if he—

"Young lady, these drawings are excellent!" Professor Rosen leaned back in his swivel chair and put his feet up on his desk. He placed Lori's portfolio carefully on a file cabinet behind him. "I would venture to say you have a bright future if you continue to learn and grow."

"Really?" Lori looked from Paul to the professor with a wide smile. "Thanks, Professor Rosen! I can't tell you how much I appreciate your looking at my work," she said sincerely.

"Well, you're certainly welcome. Tell me, have you decided you want to come to Kensington?" the professor asked.

"I'm strongly considering it."

"Excellent. You see," he went on, "Kensington's art department has a good reputation among small colleges, but I'd like to make it into one of the top programs in the country. Naturally, that means we have to attract the top high school students. So I try to catch 'em early." He grinned at Paul, who returned the grin. "Paul here is my partner in crime."

Lori was speechless. Here was the man who had written that beautiful book, one of the top people in his field, the chairman of the art and design department at Kensington College, and he was complimenting *her*—almost inviting her to come study with him.

And to think—a few short weeks ago, the very chances of her going to a prestigious school like Kensington seemed as remote as winning the lottery. But now her whole future had changed, and in less than twenty-four hours.

"Pssst!"

Danielle had been sitting across from Jack, pretending to read a book for the past twenty minutes, but her patience had finally given out. There wasn't even anyone interesting to look at because they were practically the only people there.

"Pssst!"

This time Jack lifted up his head.

"Are you thirsty? I am," she cooed, giving Jack one of her blinding smiles.

"There's a fountain down the hall," he said, immediately turning back to his book.

"But I don't want water. That's so boring. I was thinking more of Coke or something."

"There are some vending machines in the basement—right by the audio-visual section. You can't miss them," Jack said without looking up again.

"Oh. Well, you could come along and show me around the library."

Did she have to think of everything? Danielle was beginning to wonder if she might be wasting her time. Jack studied so much—maybe he was a nerd in disguise.

"Sorry, but I really can't take a break right now, Danielle," he said firmly, running his hand through his hair. "I'd love to, but I've got an exam Monday, and tonight's the party and I have to help the guys get the house ready—"

Of course! Jack had to get his work done so he could spend time with her at the party.

So he *did* like her! Hmmmm . . . she still had to get at least a couple of minutes with him right now, *before* the party. A few minutes would be all she'd need. Then he'd have all day to think about her before she showed up at the party—looking sensational.

"Well, how about if I go and get a couple of sodas and bring them back up here?"

Jack brightened immediately. "Now you're talking! Why don't you go and get them right now? Uh—don't rush, okay? I'm not going anywhere."

"Don't move," she purred softly, running her finger up his arm and dimpling at him. "I'll be back in a flash. Would you like a Coke?"

"Juice for me, if you don't mind. Oh, you'll have to go over to the student union to get it. There's no juice downstairs. Is that all right?"

"Consider it done, Jack." Danielle got up and backed toward the aisle slowly, reaching up to grab her coat off the hook behind her.

When the coat didn't budge, Danielle pulled it harder, trying to jerk it free. Thinking that the collar had probably twisted itself around the hook somehow, Danielle tugged it again—

Suddenly, instead of the coat coming free, the entire bookshelf started to tilt, and Danielle began to panic. *Those books are going to*—

As Danielle covered her face, afraid to look, hundreds of reference books cascaded off the shelves and hit the floor with a crash!

CHAPTER TEN

For a few seconds all Danielle could see was a dense cloud of dust. Where was Jack? Had she buried him alive?

"Jack! Are you all right?"

A few people wandered over from the periodicals room across the hall to see what all the noise was. The dust began to thin. Danielle let out her breath in a sigh of relief as she saw Jack's form emerge.

"No broken bones—at least I don't think so," he said as he stood up from the table and brushed himself off. "It's a good thing the library is so empty today. How about you?"

"Oh, I'm fine," Danielle said, not meeting his eyes and brushing extra long at a clump of dust on her jeans. How utterly humiliating! Here they had been on the verge of a whole new relationship, and now all Danielle's plans lay in ruins, like the musty old books on the floor around them.

"Well, we might as well pitch in," Jack mumbled when one of the librarians walked over to investigate the mess. Reaching down, he picked up a volume of the *History of Western Civilization*. "WC four-seven-three point eight-five. Let's see, that would go—up here. . . ."

Leave it to Jack to do the right thing. Now Danielle would have to get her hands dirty helping him put all the books back, or else she'd look bad. She was afraid to touch some of the books—they looked so ancient and crumbly, as if they would fall apart at any second, leaving her covered with yellow bits of paper.

Gradually, the group that had gathered at the scene managed to reshelve all the books. As soon as he put the last book back, Jack thanked everyone for helping and sat back down at the table, apparently to resume his studies. Danielle just stood there, feeling like a total idiot. No wonder he wasn't looking at her!

"You know," she said, flashing him a tremulous smile, "they really should bolt those shelves or something."

Jack didn't seem to hear her. Glancing at his watch, he whistled softly. "Danielle, I promised my frat brothers I'd get to the house in time to help with the party prep. I can't let them down."

"What about a break? Don't you ever relax?"

"Believe me, I'd love to more than anything in the world—but I just can't right now. Will you be okay?"

Danielle couldn't answer him. Her disappointment brought tears to her eyes. She had blown the whole thing, and now he hated her! She wanted to crawl under a rock—well, maybe into her nice clean bed—and die.

"Hey, it's not so bad," Jack said softly. He put a hand on her shoulder. "I *will* see you at the party tonight, won't I?"

The look in his eyes was infinitely tender. Danielle felt her spirits bloom again. He cared!

"Of course you will, Jack!" Thank goodness—he wasn't blowing her off even though she had just caused a minor disaster.

"Christine and Lori are coming too, right?" he asked.

"I don't know about Lori," Danielle hedged. "But I think Christine will be working on her term paper—it's a pretty long one, you know. She said she probably won't make it to the party."

"Oh. Well, then—I'll catch you later," said Jack, standing up. He frowned, but the look changed to a smile as he saw Danielle's heartbroken expression. He stuffed five or six books and a notebook into his knapsack and swung it over his shoulder. "Bye," he said softly as he walked under the arched entrance of the reference room.

Catch me later? Why don't you catch me now! I'm only going to be here till tomorrow! Danielle watched Jack say hello to a few people as he made his way out of the library. She followed him for a minute or two, then realized it might be a bad idea. He had to be a little angry with her—after all, she had just ruined his quiet morning of studying.

How could she ever make it up to him?

"What a gorgeous day." Lori sighed and closed her eyes, letting the unexpected warmth of the autumn sun caress her face.

"Mm-hmm," Paul's voice agreed. On their way to get Paul's design book, they had stopped at the college store to get sodas. Now they sat on the grass in the quad, enjoying the lazy feel of the day.

"You know," Paul said after a moment, "you've got an incredible profile. I'd like to draw you sometime."

Lori's eyes flew open and she blushed a fiery red. "I'll bet you say that to all the girls," she joked to cover her confusion.

Paul gave her a funny look, but then he laughed. "Every single one," he agreed. He leaned back on his elbows, looking off over the campus with half-shut eyes.

Hanging out with Paul still made Lori a little shy, but she was loving every second of it. She stole a glance at him from under her lashes. He had a very kissable mouth—

Whoa. She and Paul had never gone out on a date, never kissed, never even been totally alone together. So why did she feel as if she would do all those things with Paul if he asked her? She wouldn't hesitate for a second.

But she loved Nick, and they had something so special—she didn't want to mess that up! She wished Patsy and Ann were around to talk to. Maybe her friends could talk some sense into her and tell her to stop acting so silly.

Just then, Paul looked up and threw her a smile, and another wave of pleasure ran through her. The way he was looking at her was so intense. . . . And then suddenly Nick's face appeared before her, his blue eyes soft and loving.

"What's wrong, Lori?" asked Paul softly. "You look like you just saw a ghost."

"What? Um, nothing's wrong, I just remembered that nobody knows where I am. I should go." And she gathered herself to leave.

"Hey! Where are you going? I still haven't given you that book, remember? Anyway, nobody's running around looking for you. We're all on our own here." Paul touched her arm. "Relax!"

His touch sent ripples of warmth through Lori. *Well, why not?* she thought. *He's right. I'm free to do as I want. There's nothing to worry about. Danielle and Christine probably aren't even thinking about me, much less looking for me.*

But for the little voice that kept asking her *What about Nick?* Lori had no answer.

CHAPTER ELEVEN

Danielle stuffed the last of Christine's Belgian chocolates into her mouth and sighed. It wasn't often enough that she let herself get depressed enough to pig out, but when she did, chocolate always helped her feel better.

She felt a momentary pang of guilt at having finished the candy without asking her sister, but then she shrugged it off. After all, hadn't Christine said she was saving them for Danielle?

All right. It was time to get back into action. Somehow she had to smooth everything over with Jack so that by the party this evening he'd be putty in her hands.

Danielle stood up and smiled at herself in Christine's mirror. Then she marched out to the hall phone and dialed Sigma's number.

"Hi, this is Danielle Sharp. Is Jack there?" she asked in her sweetest phone voice. That night, she'd be meeting all of Jack's frat brothers, and she wanted them to have a favorable impression before she even walked through the door. If all his friends liked her, Jack would definitely see how great she was.

"Aldrich? Nah, he's not here. He's on lifeguard duty."

"Really?" No wonder he was in such fantastic shape. "Where?"

"At the sports center. I think there's a free swim period from three to five."

"Okay—thanks." When she put down the phone, Danielle sighed loudly. How was she ever going to get Jack alone at a pool? The library had been bad enough. Didn't he ever just stay in his room? But her frustration didn't last long. After all, Danielle Sharp was a woman of action.

Hurrying back to the room, Danielle searched her suitcases, frantically throwing clothes around the room until she found what she was looking for—her new bathing suit, a tiny electric-blue bikini.

Packing too much had its rewards, she thought happily. Between her red hair and the blue suit, she couldn't fail to win Jack Aldrich!

"What dorm are you staying in?" Paul asked as they walked down a tree-lined sidewalk toward the north end of the campus.

"Atherton," Lori answered quietly, trying to avoid his glance. She was feeling very confused—something she should be getting used to by now, she reflected wryly.

By this time tomorrow she'd be back in Merivale with Nick, safe from temptation. Nick would pick her up at the airport and Paul would start fading into memory. She'd never have to worry about seeing him again.

The question was, was she worrying—or was she hoping?

"Well, here we are," Paul suddenly announced, stopping in front of a colonial-style red brick building with dark green shutters. "We can pick up that book and then I'll walk you to Atherton. It's on my way," he added vaguely. Lori had a feeling that he wasn't really going anywhere *but* Atherton. Somehow she didn't mind.

"All right. I'll wait down here," Lori volunteered.

Paul frowned slightly. "Don't you want to come up and see my room? I was hoping you'd take a look at some of my drawings. I did a few fashion sketches freshman year. I'd like your opinion."

Lori's resolve melted. She wanted to see Paul's drawings. And after he'd spent the whole afternoon doing nice things for her, how could she possibly turn him down?

She raised her eyes to meet his. "Okay, but I really have to get back so I can—well—" She faltered. Looking into Paul's eyes always had the same effect on her: she got so flustered she couldn't finish her sentences. "I guess I told you I have work to do, and . . ." She did better when her eyes were on the ground, she decided.

As they climbed the stairs to Paul's room, Lori tried to imagine what it would look like. He was artistic: the walls were probably covered with sketches and paintings. And she had an idea there wouldn't be much else in the room except for the bare essentials.

The first thing Lori saw when Paul unlocked the door was a framed charcoal sketch hanging over his bed of what was apparently a female model. Watching Lori's gaze, Paul explained. "It was my first real drawing, so I keep it there to remind me of why I'm studying art—to get better!" He walked over to the book shelves next to his bed.

"Here it is, *A Complete History of Fashion*. Keep it as long as you want. When you're finished, you can mail it back to me. I'm not going anywhere—not till June, anyway."

"Thanks a lot," said Lori, taking the book.

"These things are old," said Paul, pulling a portfolio from under the bed. He pushed a few dustbunnies off the top before opening it. "Most of my recent stuff is over at the department." He patted the bed. "Have a seat."

Lori sat down next to Paul and flipped slowly from one drawing to the next, each flick of her wrist revealing yet another one of Paul's bold, sensitive drawings.

"These are beautiful, Paul. It's almost as though I can feel the wind blowing in this one!"

she said, indicating a stormy landscape Paul had drawn in pen and ink. "You're really talented."

"I'm glad you think so," he replied. "It means a lot coming from another artist."

An artist? Lori liked the way that sounded. Although she loved designing and sketching, she was never sure how good she was. But Paul considered her sketches art.

When she finished looking at his last drawing, she handed the portfolio to Paul and looked down, nervous about what she'd say next. Should she tell Paul how nice it had been to meet him? Or should she mention that she never knew *what* to say when he looked at her that way?

"Lori, um—I was wondering if you'd have dinner with me tonight?" Paul suddenly asked. "I know you said you had to work, but . . ."

"Oh," she said to give herself time to think. There was only one thing to do—accept his invitation, but tell him about Nick. It was only fair—to both of them.

"Paul—thank you very much, but—" She had to lift her head and look him in the eye—he had to know she was telling the truth. "You see—I, um—" *Come on, Lori! Stop stammering and get it out!* Lori took a deep breath and forced herself to look straight into Paul's beautiful blue eyes. "There's something I have to tell you."

The first thing Danielle noticed about the Kensington pool was the overpowering smell of chlorine. *Good thing I didn't waste any Fallen Angel on this*, she reflected, thinking of her perfume. At what it costs per ounce, not a drop should be wasted on a tiny school pool.

Looking around, what caught Danielle's attention next was the crowd of good-looking, muscular guys hanging out by the diving tank.

At another time she might have tried to get them to notice her. But right now, for her, only one boy existed. Coolly ignoring a group of girls glaring at her revealing bikini, Danielle carefully made her way across the wet tiled floor to the lifeguard station.

"Hello, up there!" Danielle waved to Jack from the foot of his elevated chair. "Remember me?"

Jack looked down at her and smiled. "Hi, Danielle! Decided to take a little swim?" Obviously, he had forgiven her for being such a klutz, but it also didn't look as if he were about to come down from his chair to talk to her. Danielle began to get frustrated again. Didn't he have eyes? Couldn't he see how sexy her suit was? But no, all he was looking at were the swimmers in the pool—as if one of them could actually get into trouble!

Give me a break, Danielle thought. *Nobody ever really drowns in a place like this. I mean, most of these people are at least twenty years old. They can take care of themselves!*

It was a shame that Jack was always so serious—about his studying, about his lifeguard-ing . . . even about having a party at his frat house. Didn't he ever just have *fun*?

"This place is totally outrageous!" Danielle shouted above the sounds of splashing water and people calling to one another across the pool.

Jack didn't seem to have heard her. Danielle felt a little shiver travel down her spine. He wasn't ignoring her on purpose, was he? "Wow!" she said a little louder. "This pool is super!"

This time he acknowledged her, at least. He nodded slightly in her direction, but his eyes were still busy scanning the water.

"So, how long have you been a lifeguard?" she tried again.

Jack's eyes darted from one swimmer to another. "I started when I was an eagle scout," he said.

"Well, I love the water, but I'm not such a great swimmer. Swimming is so tiring. And our pool at home is smaller than this. Maybe you could give me a lesson when you get a—"

Just then, a burly man in a red and white uniform stepped into the pool area. Jack sat up straighter in his chair. "That's my supervisor, Danielle. If he catches me talking to anybody, I'll be in big trouble."

"Oh, okay." Danielle slunk away from the chair to the edge of the pool, turning back once to see if Jack was watching her. He wasn't.

Well, if he's watching people swim, here I go! Dipping her toes into the pool, Danielle shivered. Then, tossing timidness aside, she jumped in. She threw Jack one more, slightly annoyed glance, before beginning a lazy backstroke down the pool. *I bet he pays attention only to serious swimmers*, Danielle thought. That makes sense. She headed out of the free-swim area to one of the racing lanes.

It had been a long time since she'd swum laps, but Danielle vowed to keep going until she caught Jack's eye. Once or twice she thought he was watching her, but she couldn't be sure.

On the third lap Danielle felt a prick in her side. *Rats!* She shouldn't have eaten quite so many chocolates. She hoped she wasn't going to cramp up.

Tired, she stopped stroking for a minute and let her arms hang straight down. Her head went all the way under, and for one awful second she thought she might not have the strength to lift it back up to take a breath.

She managed one quick gulp of air and struggled to continue swimming, beating her legs slowly through the water. Her whole body felt like lead, and the pain in her side was getting sharper.

Halfway to either end of the pool, and in a middle lane, Danielle suddenly realized that she wasn't going to make it. With nothing and no one to hold on to, she was going to go under— fast.

Whoosh! The water swirled in her ears and

filled her head with a giant roar as she went back under.

With her last ounce of strength, Danielle desperately tried to force her way up and cry out while waving for attention. But when she raised her arms, her head was forced down even deeper!

Where was Jack? Danielle clawed at the water and managed to lift her head one last time. *"Help!"* she screamed.

Then the pool swallowed her for the last time.

CHAPTER TWELVE

"Give her some room! She's coming to."

Danielle heard the words as if from a great distance. Slowly forcing her eyes open, she looked straight up into the blinding overhead fluorescent lights of the pool area. She snapped her lids shut and turned her head to the side. When she squinted through her lids this time, Jack Aldrich's face swayed slowly into focus.

"Jack—" she mumbled hoarsely. "Wha—what happened?"

"Shhhh—don't talk yet," came his soothing voice right beside her ear. "You got a little cramp, that's all. We got you out of the water, but you'd already fainted."

"Oh, Jack—" She looked at him tenderly. His face was no more than three inches from hers, his lips so tantalizingly close. "You saved my life—"

"Well," he said, looking down bashfully, "it *is* what I'm supposed to do. Anyway, Christine would kill me if I let anything happen to you. Are you feeling all right now?"

"I think so." Danielle almost swooned again, drowning this time in the sheer pleasure of being near him. "Yes, I'm fine, thanks to you!"

"Well, in that case—"

Don't get up, Jack—stay here with me! Danielle wanted to whisper.

"We'd better get you back to your room so you can lie down for a while," Jack said sensibly, holding her arms and helping her get to her feet.

Jack draped his towel around Danielle's shoulders and asked a girl he knew to help her get her clothes back on in the locker room. "I'll wait outside for you, okay?" he asked.

"Okay," she agreed. *Perfect!* "Thanks," she said as she followed the girl into the locker room, "but I'm all right."

It was embarrassing to have fainted in front of Jack, but he had certainly noticed her—up close and personal.

"Now I've got to get back to the house, but I want you to lie down for a while and rest," Jack warned after helping her up to Christine's room. "Maybe you ought to just stay here tonight. Socializing might be a little too much for you."

Was he crazy? Danielle wasn't going to miss that party for anything! Even if she had two broken legs, she would still drag herself across campus to be with Jack.

"I'm all right. Really—I'll be fine by tonight. Can't you stay with me just for a few more minutes? I'm not quite back to normal *yet*, you know . . ."

"I'd like to, really, but I've got to get back and help out," Jack said, moving toward the door. "Get some rest, okay?"

Just as Jack turned the knob on the door, it flew open, almost knocking him down. Christine dashed into the room, her eyes flashing with excitement. "Hi, you guys! Sorry about that, Jack—it's just that I'm in such a good mood!"

"Hello, Christine," Danielle said flatly, turning away and going to lie down on Christine's roommate's bed. Her sister's sense of timing was, as usual, dreadful.

"Christine," Jack asked, "how's the paper going? Any chance you can make it to the party tonight?"

"Surprise!" cried Christine, brandishing a paper in her hand. "I finished! Don't ask me what the paper says, but who cares? I'm going to go to the party and not even *think* about it."

Danielle's eyes opened wide and she turned her head away from the wall to stare at her sister. What terrible news!

"Hey, all *right*! That's great, Christine!" Jack said enthusiastically. Christine nodded. Her eyes were shining as she caught and held his gaze.

Just as Danielle was beginning to wonder

about the silence, Jack seemed to rouse himself. "Well, you two, it won't be much of a party if we don't get the house ready for it. So long, Danielle, and don't forget what I said! Christine, your sister had a little accident at the pool. She should take it easy tonight."

"What happened?" Christine sounded genuinely concerned.

"It was nothing, Christine. Jack just saved my life, that's all." Danielle winked at Jack.

"Well, I'll see you tonight," he said quickly, waving good-by as he slipped out the open door. *If Christine hadn't come back, he wouldn't have been so eager to leave,* Danielle complained to herself. *We'll never get any time alone!*

"Wow, Dani—are you sure you're all right?"

"I'd rather not talk about it, okay?"

Christine didn't pursue the matter any further. Obviously, she was too happy about her paper being done to care about Danielle's health.

"Here it is!" Christine announced, holding her thirty-page paper as if it were a museum piece. "It's finished, it's perfect—no typos, good footnotes—I can't believe I got it done so fast!"

Placing the paper carefully in the center of her desk, Christine jumped up and rubbed her hands together. "All right. Now I'm going to get this room cleaned up and get myself ready to party!"

She started stacking the books on her desk into three different piles. *Dull, boring, and superboring, if you ask me,* Danielle thought as she watched her sister.

Just then the door opened, and Danielle watched as Lori seemed to float in, her eyes glazed. Lori just smiled at Danielle as she slowly shrugged out of her coat.

"Hi, Lor," Christine said, wiping the dust off her desk top with a spare tissue.

"Oh, hi. What are you doing—cleaning?"

"Uh-huh."

"Want some help?"

"No, thanks, I'm fine," Christine answered cheerily. "I like cleaning up after I've finished a project. My paper's done and the only thing I have to figure out now is what to wear to the Sigma party tonight."

"Congratulations." Lori grinned at her.

"I'd help you," Danielle said weakly, "but I am feeling a little shaky after my near drowning."

"Your what?" Lori asked, shocked. "How did it happen? Are you okay?"

"I'm fine now. It was just a little cramp, but I fainted and Jack had to dive in and save me." With a sigh Danielle fluffed the pillows and leaned her head back on the bed. She didn't feel *all* that great, but she would never admit it to Lori or Christine. They'd make her stay in bed for the rest of the weekend!

"You'd better take it easy, Dani. If Mom and Dad hear what happened to you, they'll kill me." Christine laughed, hanging up some clothes in the closet. Since they had been little girls, Christine had always been the one to do all the picking up. Danielle never felt guilty about it. After all, Christine *liked* to clean, so why shouldn't Danielle let her?

"I honestly feel like I just had a thousand pounds lifted off my shoulders," Christine murmured happily, dusting her bureau.

"That's great," said Lori. "I feel pretty fantastic myself."

"I wish you'd change your mind about the party," said Christine. "It would be so much fun going with both of you. And I hate to think of you all alone up here doing your homework while we're out having a blast."

Danielle gritted her teeth. Why couldn't Christine keep her mouth shut? That was all Danielle needed. Christine *and* Lori at the dance.

Lori's cheeks turned pink before she answered her cousin. "Actually, I decided to get together with a friend tonight."

And would that friend happen to be a Kensington tour guide, Danielle wondered. Not that it mattered. As long as Lori wasn't with Danielle and Jack, she could do whatever her little heart desired.

"A friend?" Christine raised an eyebrow and shot Lori an intrigued look. "Who's this friend, Lori? What's *his* name?"

Lori's cheeks went from pink to red. "Paul Peterson. He's an art major," she replied.

"I know Paul," Christine said, shaking the

dust rag into her wastebasket. "He's a friend of my roommate's. He seems like a sweet guy."

"He is."

"Well, good for you!" Christine said, squeezing Lori's arm. She went back to her closet. "Now, you have to help me decide what to wear!"

Throwing the door of her closet open, Christine pulled out a dark green velvet miniskirt and an ivory silk blouse and held them up in front of her. "And I've got these outrageous green pumps that match my skirt! What do you think?" she asked Lori.

"That'll look amazing." Lori nodded her approval.

Christine tossed the clothes onto her bed. "Now, I think we'd better get to the bathroom before everyone else does. Saturday night is a big night for the showers around here. Danielle, you coming?"

"Oh, I'll take my chances a little later, thanks. I don't feel like getting too close to water just yet." Actually, she needed time to plan how to get Christine out of the picture.

"Okay. Here's a fresh towel, Lori." Christine tossed the towel over, then grabbed one for herself. "Let's go!" She breezed out of the room with Lori right behind her.

After they left, Danielle sat up and thought about the situation. She stood up and began pacing around the room, lightly trailing her index finger over all the newly clean surfaces as she thought. Suddenly she stopped and looked down.

In a flash, a diabolical plan took shape in her mind. She stared at Christine's paper under her finger. Her sister couldn't go out if she couldn't find her paper, now, could she? Her heart beating wildly, Danielle took a deep breath, trying to ignore her conscience. *After all*, she told herself, *all's fair in love and war!* And this was definitely a case of love!

Sorry, sis, thought Danielle, snatching the paper from the desk and stashing it in the back of Christine's closet. She stacked a few sweaters on top of it and shut the door.

"Too bad you won't be able to make the party, Christine," she said aloud. "Jack and I will miss you *terribly!*"

CHAPTER THIRTEEN

"Okay, I'm ready!" Christine turned from the makeup mirror, a cheerful expression on her face. Danielle had to admit that her sister looked sensational—the ivory silk blouse highlighted her fair skin and coppery red hair, and the green skirt fitted smoothly over her hips.

Danielle couldn't help getting a little irritated by how really terrific Christine looked in just about anything—even a faded sweat shirt and old jeans. But when she was dressed to kill, she was dazzling—so dazzling that Danielle was a tiny bit afraid to make comparisons.

"That's a great outfit," Danielle commented, not wanting to be too effusive about Christine's appearance.

"Really!" echoed Lori without a hint of jealousy. "You look incredible!"

Laughing as she adjusted one of her pearl earrings, Christine replied, "Well, it *is* a big event, you know. Danielle, you look pretty good yourself for somebody who nearly drowned two hours ago. And Lori, I love what you're wearing. I'm sure Paul will too," she said, grinning at her cousin.

Lori blushed and tugged at her navy blue and rose paisley-printed wool challis skirt. She had designed it to go with a dark blue velvet jacket that hugged her at the waist. "Thanks." She shrugged modestly. Then, glancing at her watch, she exclaimed, "Yikes! I'm supposed to be meeting Paul right now! How far is Luigi's from here, Christine? Will I be really late?"

"Mmm . . ." Christine seemed to be calculating the distance in her head. "Late enough to make an entrance but not late enough for him to think you're standing him up. The restaurant is only a five-minute walk. It's right down University Avenue, on the corner of College Boulevard. If you wait five minutes, Jack'll be here, and we can all walk with you."

Ugh. This evening was not starting out the way Danielle had hoped. Worse, Christine seemed oblivious to the fact that her term paper was missing.

"Thanks, but I don't want him to worry about me. I'd better go now," said Lori, walking to the door.

"Hey, Lori—have a good time!" Danielle sincerely hoped Lori's date went well. At least her cousin wouldn't be around messing things up that evening. Now, if Christine would just wake up and notice that her precious paper was gone!

"Yeah, have fun," Christine seconded.

"I'll try. I hope the party's great!" Lori said as she opened the door.

Once Lori was gone, Christine started putting her coat over her shoulders. Danielle began to panic. If her plan didn't work, her whole weekend at Kensington would be a complete flop.

"Ready, Danielle?"

"Almost." To stall Christine, Danielle dabbed a few more drops of Fallen Angel on her wrists and behind her ears. It was an expensive tactic, but it would be worth it if she could get her sister to stay home.

"You know, Christine," Danielle began, "I have a term paper due in a couple of weeks, and I was wondering if I, well, if I could just sneak a peek at yours. I just want to see how you did the footnotes because—"

"You want to look at my term paper *now*?" Christine interrupted. "Dani, it's almost eight o'clock!"

"Well, I don't want to read the whole thing, I'd just like to look at the way you did a couple of things. I've never done one of these really long papers before, and I'm a little nervous about it. And if I don't do well I won't get into a good college and—"

"Okay, okay, help yourself," said Christine,

standing in the doorway with a perplexed look on her face.

"Thanks. Where is it, anyway?" Danielle's eyes widened innocently.

"It's right on my desk."

"Where? I don't see it." Danielle threw her hands up. "Did you put it under these books?"

"No! It's right in the mid—hey, where is it?" Christine asked, obviously realizing that her desk was completely clear and that her term paper was missing in action. She joined Danielle at the desk and frantically said, "I put it right here! Don't you remember?"

"You did?"

"Yes! I came in, and I said 'thank goodness I finished this' and I put it *right here*."

A look of panic had replaced Christine's happy expression. "What did I do with it after that?" she muttered.

Danielle tried to look worried. "Gosh, maybe when you cleared the room you moved it somewhere else. Maybe it just fell into the wastebasket or something," Danielle suggested, fully aware that Christine had emptied the trash into a garbage chute in the hallway during her cleaning spree.

Christine's hand flew to her mouth. "No! I *couldn't* have thrown it out—could I?" She looked down into the wastebasket. "It's empty! Oh, no—I already dumped it! What am I going to do?"

"You wouldn't have thrown it out," said

Danielle, biting her cheek so she wouldn't break out in a smile. "You're too neat for that. I bet you put it in a drawer or something."

Five minutes later Christine's room looked like a burglar had been at work. Every drawer was pulled out. Christine sat on the bed holding her head in her hands.

"I can't believe this," she moaned. "I must have thrown it down the chute. My term paper is probably in the incinerator as we speak."

"Knock, knock. Can I come in?"

Standing in the open doorway, Jack looked like he had just stepped out of a men's fashion magazine. He wore a crisp white shirt under a double-breasted charcoal gray wool suit, and his wavy dark hair was swept back off his forehead. Danielle thought she might die. *He looks so collegiate. I wish Teresa and Heather could see him.*

"Jack, you're not going to believe this." Tears stood in Christine's eyes as she explained what had happened. "I can't believe I did something so stupid! That's the most important paper I had to write all semester!"

For a moment Danielle felt bad for her sister, but then she pulled herself together. Christine liked to work—she'd probably even have fun redoing the paper. And when she saw what a great couple Jack and Danielle were going to make, she'd be glad she'd let them have this night alone together.

"Okay, let's not panic," said Jack in a cool, take-charge voice. "Did you make a copy of it?"

Darn, Danielle thought. *I didn't think of that.*

"No, I always wait until just before I hand it in," Christine answered.

Danielle stifled a sigh of relief.

"Well," Jack went on, "did you lose your notes?"

Christine jumped up and went to her book bag hanging on the back of her desk chair. "No, they're all in here."

"Well," Jack said, "I hate to tell you this, but if you start now, you'll probably be able to reconstruct the paper. I bet you'll remember a lot of it as you go along."

"What a bummer! Does that mean you can't come with us to the party?" Danielle asked, trying her hardest to sound genuinely worried. "Can't you write it tomorrow?"

"No." Christine looked miserable. "Tomorrow I've got a big test to study for. I'll be up all night rewriting the thing," she moaned.

Again Danielle felt a little prick of remorse. But then she looked over at Jack, and her misgivings disappeared. She would make it up to Christine someday. Just not tonight.

"I'll stay and help you with it," Jack offered gallantly.

Oh, no! Danielle hadn't considered Jack's volunteering to help—she hoped Christine would realize he was only being polite.

Christine looked so happy at Jack's offer

that for a moment Danielle's heart stood in her mouth. She was going to accept!

Then Christine shook her head. "Don't be silly, Jack. There's no sense in *two* people staying in on a Saturday night. Besides, it's my paper and I'm the one who threw it out. No, you guys go ahead and have a good time. Just think of me once in a while, okay?" And with a sad smile she started reviewing her notes. "Oh, good—here's a rough outline," she said, distracted.

Masking her happiness with a depressed look, Danielle walked up to Jack, possessively looped her arm through his, and shepherded him out the still-open door. "Come on," she said softly, "we'd better let her be. Bye, Christine! Hope it won't take *too* long to rewrite your paper."

Not too long—just long enough for me to hook and land Jack Aldrich!

"Hey, Jack. Aren't you going to introduce me to your friend?" a tall guy with curly black hair asked, staring at Danielle as she and Jack stood in the doorway of the fraternity house.

Jack stopped to help Danielle off with her coat. "Danielle Sharp, this is Drew Cooper. Danielle is visiting for the weekend. Maybe you can show her around while I set up the punch and check out the tape situation with Tony."

Jack turned to Danielle and smiled warmly. "I hope that's okay with you, Danielle. I sort of promised to co-host the party, and I'm going to be pretty busy, at least for the first hour."

Too shocked to answer, Danielle felt a hand on her elbow as Drew guided her into the main room. She looked at Jack, who was behind them. How could he leave her with this bozo? Didn't he realize this was their last night together?

"Oh, don't worry, Jack," Drew said. "I'll take good care of Danielle. After all, what are fraternity brothers for? Come on, Danielle—I'll show you around."

"I *will* see you later, right?" Danielle asked Jack, pulling her arm free from Drew's sweaty palm.

"For sure," he replied with a small smile. Then he did something that made Danielle's heart stop—he leaned closer and gave her a kiss on the cheek. "Have a good time. See you later."

"I knew this would be a great night," she murmured as Jack walked away. Here she was, standing in a college fraternity house with good-looking boys surrounding her, and her favorite one of all had just kissed her . . . she'd miss Jack, but the wait would be worth it!

"Hey, Drew! What's up?" Two good-looking guys walked up to Danielle and Drew the minute they appeared in the large party room.

"Okay, I know you guys are talking to me for only one reason," Drew said. "This is Danielle. She's a friend of Aldrich's, actually. I wish I could say she came with me. Mademoiselle Sharp, this is Chip, and this is John."

"Well, Danielle, would you like to dance?" Chip asked. When Danielle agreed, he took her hand and led her out onto the dance floor, where several couples were moving to the music.

What an improvement over the boys at Atwood! These Kensington guys were sophisticated and witty. They were smart, rich, and well-dressed too—and they were almost all hunks!

Guys like Nick Hobart and Ben Frye—the Atwood catches—looked like nothing more than little boys in comparison. And as for someone like Don James, well, he and Danielle were ancient history at this point. Kensington College was where she belonged.

And later, when things quieted down, and Jack had some time to be with her, she'd dance with *him*, the guy she had come all the way to Kensington to conquer.

CHAPTER FOURTEEN

Lori and Paul stepped out of Luigi's into the night. The weather had gotten increasingly humid and foggy, and as they emerged, Paul draped Lori's coat around her shoulders. "Wind's picking up," he said, almost nuzzling her ear. "Looks like a storm brewing."

"Yes, it does." Distant thunder rolled across the far hills, echoing softly in the night. But the real storm was brewing in Lori Randall's heart. All through dinner Lori had tried to tell Paul about Nick, but each time something had stopped her. Deep down, she wanted this crazy adventure to continue.

"Feel like taking a little walk? The storm's still far off, and I don't know about you, but I could use the exercise. Italian food is heavy."

"Mmmm, I know, but it was delicious." Lori sighed happily.

Paul reached for Lori's hand, and his warm fingers closed around hers. Lori knew she was in trouble. Holding Paul's hand seemed so natural, it was scary. They strolled down one tree-lined avenue after another, and as they walked, she let her head rest on his shoulder.

"You know, Paul," she said thoughtfully, "I've always wanted, more than anything, to feel like—like, well—somebody special. A real artist, a fine designer, somebody with an exciting future. That's how I feel when I'm with you."

"You're incredibly special, Lori," he said, dropping her hand to wrap his arm around her shoulder. "I can't believe you don't know that already."

"Paul—" Lori sighed. "There's something I've been meaning to tell you all night. It's been on my mind, and—"

A deafening clap of thunder cut Lori's sentence in half. Lori jumped in fright, and Paul drew her close.

"Maybe we should start heading back to your dorm," he said just as a bolt of lightning lit up the sky. "Do I make my point?" He laughed.

They turned up the next street, walking faster and faster as the lightning and thunder grew nearer.

"Lori," Paul said as they hurried up a hill hand in hand, "now that you've seen Kensington, do you think you'd like to come here?"

"Oh, yes! Yes, I would. It's everything I dreamed it would be." *And more*—that was the problem. She'd never dreamed there'd be a Paul Peterson and that life could be so complicated.

"I'm glad," he said, smiling. "I think it would be a terrific place for you."

"You do?" Lori held her breath.

"Well—I'd like to see more of you." He stopped and looked into her eyes. "A lot more."

Boom!!! The sky was lit up for a second with blinding white light, and then huge raindrops began pelting them.

"We'd better really run for it now!" Paul yelled, grabbing her hand and leading her down the street toward the campus.

"Aaahhhh!!" screamed Lori, laughing as she ran, her wet hair plastered to her rain-drenched face. Water squished in her shoes with every step.

"Come on! Let's duck in here!" Paul gestured toward a covered doorway with his head, and they veered under its shelter.

"I can't believe this!" Lori laughed, trying to catch her breath. "You're soaked, Paul—I can only imagine what *I* look like!"

Paul brushed a few strands of hair back from Lori's face. "You look fantastic," he said quietly. And cupping his hands around her shoulders, he pulled her gently toward him and brushed her lips lightly with his.

Shivering with excitement, Lori put all of her tumbling and confused emotions out of her head and kissed Paul back with all the passion of the moment. As the rain poured down around them, she and Paul clung together as if they had been apart for months.

Finally Lori pulled away and opened her eyes. She looked dreamily at Paul.

"Wow," Paul said, caressing her dripping hair and looking at her as if he were gazing right into her soul. "I've been wanting to do that all evening."

He touched her cheek with one finger. "A few minutes ago you said there was something *you'd* been waiting to tell *me*. What was it, Lori?"

"Oh, nothing. Nothing important." Lori smiled up at Paul.

"Good." Paul leaned over as he drew her to him again, his lips caressing her face and finding her mouth in another fervent kiss.

Happy and exhausted, Danielle twirled across the dance floor for what felt like the hundredth time. Her partner this time was a guy named Freddy, who danced with a wild abandon Danielle wouldn't have expected from his quiet, almost stiff demeanor.

"So listen," he said when the music stopped, "it's kind of late. People seem to be taking off. But do you want to go out for some coffee or something?"

Danielle had loved all the attention from Jack's frat brothers, but now it was time for Jack himself—and only Jack. "Sorry, but I came with a date." A date she hadn't gotten to dance with *once*, she thought unhappily. "In fact, I'd better go find him now. But thank you anyway."

Danielle made her way across the dance floor to the far end of the room where she had last seen Jack, at the punch bowl.

But another guy was standing behind the refreshment table. Well, that meant Jack was probably getting their coats so they could leave. Any minute now she'd be walking out the door on the arm of the most sophisticated and intelligent guy she'd ever met.

"Hi," Danielle said. "Do you know where Jack Aldrich is?"

The boy looked puzzled. "I saw him a while ago. I think he was helping with the tapes or something. You might check over there." He pointed to the other end of the room where the stereo system was located.

Danielle hurried to the spot, but the guy manning the music table didn't know where Jack was either. "Did you ask the guys in the kitchen? Maybe he went in there for a break," he suggested.

Her heart pounding under her white silk dress, Danielle walked into the kitchen. There were five guys standing around dunking doughnuts into huge glasses of milk. Danielle recognized some of her dance partners from earlier in the evening. "A little midnight snack," one of them explained.

"Is Jack Aldrich around?" asked Danielle, trying to cover the growing frustration in her voice. All the guests were gone except for her, and these guys were acting like the party was over. Well, it might be over for them, but Danielle and Jack still had a date ahead of them!

The boys looked confused for a moment. Finally one of them shrugged and said, "Sorry. Haven't seem him."

Just then, the short, young-looking boy who had been behind the drinks table entered the kitchen. "You're looking for Jack Aldrich, right?" he asked.

Thank goodness! He was probably hunting for her just like she was hunting for him!

"Yes, that's right. Where is he?"

"Tony just told me Jack took off about an hour ago—he wanted to help a friend of his study for an exam or something," the boy explained. "But he asked if one of us would walk Danielle back to the dorm, because she's a visiting high school student and he didn't want her to get into any trouble."

Danielle's cheeks felt as if they were on fire. "It's okay—Danielle can get back on her own," she said, furious.

Not only had Jack stood her up, he had completely humiliated her by telling his frat brothers she was still in high school!

Well, she *might* forgive him—*if* he made it up to her. Pushing the swinging doors of the kitchen, she stomped into the front hall to pick up her coat.

As she stepped out the front door, Danielle noticed that it had been raining. Funny, she'd been so busy dancing she hadn't even noticed.

Clouds were breaking up and a full moon was emerging in the night sky. He left to help some guy study in the middle of a party? That was certainly carrying friendship a bit too far! The more she thought about it, the angrier Danielle became.

By the time she got back inside the lobby of the dorm, hot tears were stinging Danielle's cheeks. *How dare he abandon her!* Danielle ran up the single flight of stairs to the second floor, moving as fast as she could in her silk dress and low heels. She had done so much for Jack, and he had treated her like a . . . like a *nobody*! It was humiliating!

She hesitated in front of Christine's room. She didn't want to have to explain why she was so upset, so she took a deep breath and wiped the tears off her cheeks. Slowly, she turned the doorknob and pushed open the door.

Christine wasn't at her desk, and Danielle peeked around the edge of the doorknob and pushed the door to see if she was over by the closet.

What Danielle saw next made her wish she'd never even *heard* of Kensington College. There, right in front of her, Christine was locked in a passionate embrace—with none other than Jack Aldrich!

CHAPTER FIFTEEN

This can't be happening.

Quickly turning around and running out the door, Danielle fled back down the stairs and out of the dormitory. She stood outside for a minute, wondering what to do next. *Where do I go?* she asked herself wildly.

Suddenly she knew—the student union, where the snack bar stayed open until three in the morning. Danielle needed a place where she could sit, collect her thoughts, and stuff her face.

Walking into the brightly lit green room, Danielle picked up an apple turnover from the stainless steel counter and paid for it at the register. Then she headed straight for the rear of the deserted room. As she walked between Formica-topped tables and molded plastic chairs, she kept her eyes on her feet, hoping she wouldn't run into any of Jack's frat brothers.

Looking up to take a seat, she noticed a

solitary figure huddled in front of a table, her head resting in her hands.

"Lori! What are you doing here?" Danielle asked, shocked at Lori's appearance. Her hair was matted down, and her eye makeup had streaked all over her cheeks. Danielle set her plate on the table and pulled up a chair. She sat down across from Lori and peered at her cousin's unhappy face.

"Lori, what's the matter? Did you get caught in the rain, or have you been crying?" Danielle asked.

"Oh! Danielle—I feel like my whole life is falling apart!"

"What happened? Was it your date?" Danielle's eyes narrowed. "Did that guy Paul do something?"

"No, not really. I mean, he was *wonderful*— *that's* the problem!"

"Huh?" Lori had Nick Hobart at home and a terrific college guy here, and she had *problems*? Danielle had to hear this.

"Oh, Danielle—tonight was one of the most perfect nights I've ever had . . . and I'm miserable. I just can't decide who I really love—Paul or Nick! They're both so sweet, they're both so fantastic, but how can I love them both! What's wrong with me?"

"There's nothing the matter with you, Lori," Danielle said. She meant it. Lori could be an all-right person most of the time. "You want it all, you should have it all."

"What, you mean go out with both of them?" Lori asked incredulously.

"It has happened once or twice down through the ages," Danielle replied lightly, taking a bite of her turnover. "It's called playing the field."

"Wow, I don't think I could handle that," Lori sighed.

"Well, as long as you don't tell either one of them about the other, there's really nothing to handle, now, is there?" Danielle said in a matter-of-fact voice. "Listen, Lori, anytime you'd like to switch problems, I'm game."

"Really? Oh, Danielle, I'm sorry. I'm so wrapped up in my *own* situation that I didn't even think about yours. Forgive me, okay?"

"It's all right." Danielle bit her lip. She had forgotten her own miserable situation for a minute. But now that Lori had asked, the torrent of hurt and betrayal came flooding back into her mind.

"The rat," she fumed, shaking her head angrily as she pictured Jack and Christine kissing. "He was two-timing me with my own sister!"

"Who?" Lori looked startled.

"Jack, of course! Can you believe it? I walked into the room, and he was kissing Christine! And this was supposed to be *our* big night together too! You were there when he asked me, weren't you?"

"Wait a minute, Danielle, I thought Jack invited all of us to the dance," Lori pointed out.

"Lori, he asked you and Christine only because he was being polite. He really wanted me to go with him, as his date!"

Lori was silent for a minute. Then she said, "Maybe you misread his signals, Danielle. Maybe he wanted to show us a good time because we were Christine's guests. You know, he could have invited us because he wanted to impress *her*."

Danielle opened her mouth to tell Lori not to be ridiculous. But then, slowly, she closed it again. She thought of the way Jack always seemed to bring up Christine's name in conversations. And the way he'd kept asking if Christine was going to come to the Sigma party.

Lori's comments suddenly made a lot of sense to Danielle. But if Lori was right, Danielle was totally confused!

Why were college kids so strange? Why did they study so much? And why did they act like they liked a girl when they were really interested in her sister?

"Oh, Lori," she moaned, "I feel like such a fool!" She threw her turnover down on her tray, too heartsick to eat any more.

Lori reached out for Danielle's hand. For the first time on this trip, Danielle was glad her cousin was there. Lori was somebody she could relate to, somebody from her own world, with her own values—more or less.

"How could he pass me up for Christine? How, Lori?" Danielle asked, willing herself not to cry.

It wasn't the kind of question that required an answer. Lori propped her chin on her hands and leaned forward. "Feel like talking about it some more?" she prompted.

"I made a fool out of myself for that jerk," Danielle confessed, a teardrop slipping out of her eye. She wiped it away angrily. "A complete fool!"

"No, you didn't!" protested Lori. "Just because you like someone and they don't like you back doesn't mean you're foolish."

"Okay, then it means I was stupid!"

"Come on, Danielle, I was there with you and Jack. And I know Jack likes you. Maybe he's just not interested—romantically. He and Christine have a lot in common. They like a lot of the same classes, they're both sophomores in college. . . ."

"It's because I'm still in high school, isn't it?" Danielle concluded. "He thinks I'm a nice kid, and that's it! Oh, I could just die—"

"Dani," Lori said, "I hate to see you so upset."

"Want to know the worst part? He's right! I really am just a high school kid!" Danielle's shoulders slumped despairingly.

"Danielle," Lori said softly, "there's nothing wrong with that. Most of these kids are only a couple of years older than we are—and they were all in high school once too, you know! Don't be in such a hurry to graduate. We'll be in college soon enough.

"Anyway," she added, "in that fantastic dress, I'll bet you made as big a hit as any college girl could have."

Danielle brightened. It was true—she *had* made a splash, if the opinions of half the Sigma brothers were worth anything. "Yeah," she said, grinning. Then she sobered again. "But this has still been the worst weekend of my entire life," she complained. "Believe me."

"Well, maybe you should look at it another way," Lori suggested. "You learned a lot about college life in the last two days. When you're a freshman, you'll be two days ahead of everyone else."

Danielle stared at her cousin. Sometimes she couldn't help being amazed at how much Lori had grown up.

"Thanks, Lor," she said, smiling sincerely. "I like the sound of that." Suddenly she felt a wave of warmth for her cousin. "Listen, when we're back in Merivale, we'll see more of each other, okay?"

Lori's eyes were shining. "I like the sound of that!"

CHAPTER SIXTEEN

"Lori, it's such a beautiful day, don't you think?"

Christine sat opposite Lori in the dining hall, playing idly with the French toast on her plate.

"And last night was so wonderful too!"

"Oh?" Lori mumbled, eating a spoonful of cereal. She could guess the reason behind Christine's exuberant mood, but she didn't want to betray Danielle's confidence. She tried not to show any emotion. "Did you get your paper done?"

Christine's face darkened for a moment. "Well, no, but I got the first few pages rewritten and I think I'll be able to finish it today—if I can keep my mind on my work, that is." She paused and a dreamy smile played over her lips. "You know what? I think I'm in love!"

"In love?" Lori asked, looking innocent.

"Yes—with Jack Aldrich! It's so funny—I've

been interested in him for a while now, and apparently he's liked me, too, but we were both so busy trying to impress each other that neither of us ever picked up on each other's signals. I didn't think he liked me!"

"Really?" Lori said. She'd suspected something like that was happening.

"Mm-hm. I feel great!" Christine stretched luxuriously. "Remember what it was like when you and Nick first got together? Wasn't it the best day of your life?"

Lori dropped her spoon at the mention of Nick's name, splashing her blouse with milk from her cereal. Hastily, she dabbed at the spots with a napkin.

"Did I say something I shouldn't have?" asked Christine.

"Not really," Lori sighed. "It's just that—remember the date I went on last night?"

"What's the matter, didn't it turn out well?"

"Oh, Christine—I'm supposed to be in love with Nick, right? And then Paul comes along and knocks me right off my feet. But if I'm in love with one guy, how could I fall for a different one?"

"It happens." Christine laughed. "Both my roommates went through it last year. Besides, you're sixteen years old, Lori—it's okay to like more than one guy."

Lori shifted uncomfortably in her chair. She had always believed in ideal love—one guy, forever and ever. And when she found Nick, she had thought that was it. She still was crazy about him, but now there were *two* guys, and she wasn't so sure about the forever and ever part either.

"Look." Christine leaned forward. "You're leaving for Merivale today. That sort of puts Paul in the background, doesn't it? And if you wind up coming to Kensington someday, well, you can deal with that then."

"I can't just *not* see Paul all that time!" Lori moaned. "And I'm going to have to tell Nick all about what happened. He'll probably break up with me as soon as I do. Then I'll have nobody."

"Hey, Lori, calm down," her cousin advised. "First things first. Does Paul know about Nick?"

Lori shook her head.

"I see." Christine nodded. "Well, you know what they say—honesty is the best policy. I believe it. Look, tell everyone the truth, and then let your heart figure out which boy is the right one for you. That's my advice, anyway, for what it's worth."

Lori stood up and kissed her cousin on the cheek. "It's worth a whole lot. Thanks, Christine."

"Where are you going?"

"To Paul's dorm. I've got to go say good-by, anyway, and now's as good a time as any to tell him about Nick—while I've still got the nerve." She plucked her jacket off the back of her chair.

"Good luck, Lori."

"Thanks. I'll need it."

* * *

Danielle listlessly folded her blue and green Norwegian ski sweater and tossed it into her suitcase. In spite of her talk with Lori last night, she still felt really down. The weekend had been an absolute disaster.

After the accident in the library, the scene in the pool, and Jack's callous abandonment of her at the Sigma party last night, she was sure she was the laughingstock of the entire campus. She could only pray that word of it didn't get back to Atwood! Heather and Teresa would jeer her out of existence if they ever found out. . . .

Oh, well. Danielle moved over to the closet to get her silk dress. She'd deal with Heather and Teresa when the time came. After all, Danielle Sharp could handle anything, couldn't she?

As Danielle pulled the dress off the rack, she remembered Christine's paper, hidden on the shelf above her head. *I suppose I might as well give it back*, she thought. *A lot of good it did me!*

She reached up and took the paper down. But as she did so, she heard the door to Christine's room opening, and then—oh, no!—the sound of Jack Aldrich's voice! She froze with her hand in midair. She couldn't face Jack and Christine right now! *Please go away*, she begged silently.

"Boy, am I glad I ran into you," Jack was

saying, his voice soft and intimate. "I haven't seen you since last night, you know—I was beginning to feel deprived!"

Oh, yuck. Danielle cringed.

"Mmmm, me too," Christine answered. "But we'll have to be miserable a little longer, I'm sorry to say—I've still got to finish this paper."

"All right, I guess I can survive until this evening. But you've got to have dinner with me," Jack said.

"It's a deal. Hey, I wonder where Danielle is? She was still sleeping when I went to breakfast."

That's what you think, Danielle grumbled mentally. She had hardly slept all night, but she'd pretended to be off in dreamland so that she wouldn't have to talk to Christine about Jack.

"Well, it's a pretty safe bet she's not at the pool or the library," Jack said with a laugh. "Poor Danielle. I hope she had a good time this weekend in spite of all that stuff. She's a great kid, you know. I like her."

Great kid? Danielle began to steam again. If Jack Aldrich was so dense he didn't know a woman of the world when he saw one, she was glad to be rid of him. She didn't want an idiot for a boyfriend!

"Yeah, Danielle is one of a kind. I think she's great too," Christine was saying. "Look, I'll come by the library around six-thirty and pick you up, okay? Now, go away. But first"— she put on a foreign accent—"kiss me, you fool!"

There was a short silence, and then the sound of a door closing.

Danielle's arm was beginning to ache. Cautiously, she lowered it to her side, then shifted her foot slightly.

Crash! Danielle squeezed her eyes shut. What had she kicked over—it sounded like a box full of pots and pans!

When she opened her eyes, Christine was standing at the closet door, staring at her. "Dani!" her sister exclaimed. "What are you doing there?"

Danielle summoned a weak smile. "Just packing up," she said. Trying to seem unconcerned, she stepped out of the closet and looked blandly at her sister.

"Were you standing there the whole time Jack and I were talking?" Christine demanded. "That's eavesdropping!"

"No, it's not," Danielle objected, her anger flaring again. "Can I help it if you and Mr. Wonderful can't stop acting sappy all the time? 'I'm beginning to feel deprived,' " she said, mimicking Jack. "You don't think I *wanted* to listen to that, do you?"

"Danielle!" Christine looked shocked—and hurt. "I thought you'd be happy for me."

"Right—for the sister who ruined my weekend!" Danielle knew she didn't really mean that, but she couldn't stop herself. "You just stood there and watched me make a fool of myself over *your* boyfriend!"

"What are you talking about?" Christine asked sharply.

"You knew I liked him," Danielle ranted on, ignoring Christine's astonished expression, "and you never said a word about liking him yourself! I never knew you were so mean, Christine.

"Well, *here*." Danielle was really working herself up. Christine just stood there, the color completely gone from her face. "Just to show you that *I'm* not vindictive." She thrust the thirty-page paper at her sister. "I didn't have to give you this, you know."

"My paper!" Christine seemed to be reeling. "Where did you find it?"

"Where I put it, of course."

"You mean, you—you *stole* this from me deliberately?" Christine looked as if she were about to strangle Danielle. "I can't believe it!"

"What was I supposed to do? It was the only way I could spend any time alone with Jack without you hanging around! And, as you already know, my plan had completely the *opposite* effect. I was going to give it back to you today anyway."

"Do you realize how much extra work you put me through? I could scream!" Christine seethed.

"*You* could scream? You're the one who wound up with Jack. But I should have expected that, I suppose. You've always gotten the best stuff."

As soon as Danielle said that, she knew she'd gone too far. There was a silence. Then, in a quiet voice, Christine asked, "What do you mean by that?"

All of a sudden Danielle was horrified to feel tears filling her eyes. "Nothing," she said.

"Danielle, I know you didn't just say that by accident. What are you talking about?"

Danielle took a deep breath. "All right, you asked," she said, trying to keep her voice steady. "Life is so easy for you, Christine. You *always* look great. You *always* get good grades. Mom never nags you about anything. She saves it all for *me*!

"All I ever hear at home is 'Christine did that,' or 'Christine would never have done this.' Well, I'm sorry if I'm not as perfect as you, but there's nothing I can do about it!" A sob shook Danielle, and suddenly scalding tears were spilling down her cheeks.

"Oh, Dani." Danielle felt Christine's arms around her shoulders. "Is that really what you think? That I'm some kind of legend you have to live up to?"

Danielle couldn't speak. She just nodded, trying to blot her tears with her silk dress.

"You're wrong, you know. Life isn't easy for me any more than it is for you. You think Mom never nags me? You should hear what I have to put up with."

Danielle took a tissue from Christine's desk and blew her nose. "Like what?" she asked, curious in spite of herself.

"Oh, you know—'Christine, I just don't understand why you don't have a boyfriend.' 'Christine, why didn't you try for an Ivy League college?' 'Christine, why don't you come home more often?' "

Danielle laughed shakily. It sounded so much like what their mother said to her!

Christine looked into Danielle's eyes. "It isn't you," she said gently. "It's Mom. Let's face it, she's not happy unless she's picking on someone. You just happen to be handy, that's all."

"So why doesn't it get to you the way it gets to me?" Danielle wanted to know.

"It does! I guess I just found a different way of dealing with it. You're rebelling against it—I accepted it. I spent a lot of my life trying to please Mom—by doing well in school, by being everybody's friend. But you know what? When I did one thing right, she'd find another thing to complain about. So finally I just stopped worrying about it."

Danielle drew in a long breath. "I guess that's what I have to do too," she said.

Christine nodded. "That, or just convince Mom you've suddenly gone deaf."

"No way. She'd just learn sign language," Danielle cracked. "Picture that!"

They looked at each other and burst out laughing. "Oh, Dani," Christine exclaimed, hugging her, "I'm really glad you're my sister!"

Danielle hugged Christine back. "Me too," she said. "Me too."

CHAPTER SEVENTEEN

Lori hurried across the north end of campus toward Paul's dorm, and with every step her resolve grew greater. She was going to tell him about Nick—gently, of course.

It was going to be hard to talk seriously to Paul when what she really wanted was for him to hold her close and kiss her. But she had mustered up the courage, and she wasn't going to stop now.

But stop she did, right outside the dorm. There was Paul, seated on a wooden bench—talking to a beautiful girl. He was holding her hand and laughing, and gazing at her with a lot more like love than friendship in his blue eyes.

Lori felt as if someone had punched her in the stomach. Paul was looking at that girl exactly as he had looked at her last night—as if she were the most special person in the world and no one else could even come close. And from the way the girl was gradually edging her way closer to Paul, it was clear that the feeling was mutual.

Paul put his hands on the girl's shoulders and gave them a squeeze. Lori had to shut her eyes. He was going to kiss her! That was the same move he had used the night before with Lori.

With a gasp Lori turned away and started walking. She never thought she'd use the word *move* to describe Paul—he didn't seem like that type of guy. But she had obviously been wrong about him—very wrong. She wanted to run as far away as she could, away from Paul Peterson and Kensington College and all the wonderful and terrible feelings the whole weekend had brought up in her.

"Lori! Hey, wait up!" Paul's gentle voice called to her from across the quad. She turned and saw him waving good-by to the other girl. Then he hurried toward Lori. "You're leaving at noon, aren't you? Don't you even want to say good-by?" he asked.

"Oh, I certainly do!" Lori burst out, barely managing to hold back her tears.

"Lori, what's wrong?"

Paul stared into Lori's eyes. He seemed concerned about her, but was it all just an act, she wondered. Had he been pretending to like her the whole time?

"Isn't it obvious what's wrong?" she asked.

"Listen, Lori—I'm sorry you showed up at

an awkward moment, but honestly, it's no big deal."

"Well," Lori stammered, "you and that girl were—were—holding hands. . . ."

"And . . . ?"

"And, I thought after last night, I thought you and I—well, that we had something special, and that we were serious about each other."

"Serious? But Lori, we've known each other for only two days. How can we possibly be serious so soon?"

Lori didn't know what to say. Everything he said made sense, but if he didn't care about her, why had he kissed her?

"That girl happens to be a very good friend of mine. I enjoy spending time with her just as I enjoyed spending it with you. It doesn't mean I like you any less.

"There are lots of great people in the world," Paul continued, "and I want to get to know quite a few of them."

Lori sifted through Paul's logic. As hard as she tried to understand him, it didn't make sense—not to her.

"We're both young, there's so much ahead of us—" he said. But that didn't explain anything as far as Lori was concerned. That was beside the point.

The more Paul spoke, the more she decided that she didn't agree with him. Could it be that Paul just wasn't the right guy for her after all?

She and Paul were looking for two very different things. Paul wanted to see a lot of different girls and get to know them all. But for Lori, playing the field didn't feel right. To him a kiss was just a kiss—to Lori a kiss was a kind of pledge. A pledge that meant, you mean something special to *me*, and you come first with me. A pledge of fidelity.

And as soon as she possibly could she intended to give that pledge to the real guy in her life. Nick Hobart!

"So, come on, Lori—tell all! Did you meet any devastating college guys?" Ann Larson's gray eyes sparkled with curiosity.

"And did you give them all my phone number?" Patsy Donovan asked. It was Sunday night, and the three of them were walking down the promenade of Merivale Mall on their way to the SixPlex.

But Lori, looking from one of them to the other, merely shook her head and said, "It was pretty boring. You guys don't really want to hear about it."

"Boring!" cried Patsy. "Randall, we know you're holding out on us. What happened?"

Lori stared silently at a shop window as they passed by, ignoring Patsy's question.

"You *did* meet somebody!" Ann exclaimed.

Lori smiled at Ann. She'd have to tell them sooner or later. "All right," she began, "but it's a long story. Much longer and more complicated than I want to get into right now. Let's just say, whatever happened, it's over now. I'm back in Merivale, still going out with Nick, still a high school junior, and happy about all three. College is something I'm definitely not ready for yet—not by a long shot."

"Are you going to tell Nick?" Patsy asked.

Lori gazed down the promenade in the direction of Hobart Electronics, Nick's father's store. "Yes, I'm going to tell him—everything," she said quietly.

"Don't worry, Lori. Whatever happens with you and Nick, we're with you all the way," said Ann. "Besides, I'm sure he'll understand."

"You two will work it out," Patsy agreed confidently. "Don't ask me why. But the guy seems to be crazy about you. I'm sure *I* can't understand it," she joked.

"And I actually missed you while I was gone!" Lori shook her head, laughing.

"Hey—don't forget, absence is supposed to make the heart grow fonder," Ann reminded them.

"Okay, okay." Patsy reached over and put her arm around Lori's shoulder. "Now, what *really* happened?"

"So, Red—heard you went to college for the weekend. When's the wedding?"

Don James's gaze challenged Danielle from the doorway of the Video Arcade. *The nerve of him*, Danielle thought as she strode purposefully away. *The absolute nerve!*

"Hey! Where you going?" he called out, hurrying after her. She picked her pace up slightly, rolling her eyes in annoyance.

"Don, please leave me alone!" she demanded. "I've got important things on my mind."

"Leave you alone? No problem. Now that you've hobnobbed with all those fancy college guys, you're too good to even *talk* to a grease monkey like me. Am I close?"

Danielle didn't answer right away. He was right—sort of. On the one hand, she was too good for an auto mechanic, but on the other hand, Don *was* gorgeous . . . and witty . . . and kind . . . and—here!

Don stood opposite her, sizing her up. "Red, I don't want to rain on your parade or anything, but this college boy of yours—whoever he is, and don't deny there is one—will probably forget all about you before you can say S.A.T. You know, out of sight, out of mind? Then you'll probably run right back to me."

That was the problem with Don James. He always knew what Danielle was thinking, what was bothering her. "Don James, I wouldn't go out with you if you were the last guy on earth!" she maintained, praying he hadn't heard about her disastrous weekend.

"Okay by me!" He shrugged. "But if—that is, *when*—you change your mind, I don't know if I'll be available! I may be all booked up, so don't forget to, ah, RSVP," he said in a snobby tone.

That does it! she thought, turning and walking away. If he's going to make fun of me, I'm not even talking to him.

Then she slowed down. She thought about how sweet and understanding Don really could be. *Maybe I will call him later. It won't hurt to keep him on the line. No one else has to know*, she decided.

Danielle turned to face Don and impulsively threw him a dazzling smile. He winked, and she knew the chase was still on.

Even if Don wasn't exactly right for her, he would do until someone perfect came along. And Danielle knew that just around the corner, Mr. Right was waiting for her. It was only a matter of time.